"So, Mr. Novak. Have you ever thought about donating your sperm to a good cause?"

"Excuse me?" Yaeger asked.

"Your sperm," Hannah said, enunciating the word more clearly this time. "Have you ever thought about donating it?"

"Uh...no."

"I mean, if you would consider it—donating it to me, I mean—I'd sign any kind of legal documents you want to relieve you of all obligations for any offspring that might, um, you know, spring off me. I'd really appreciate it."

"Hannah, I...I'm flattered, but it's not a good idea for me to do something like that."

She looked crestfallen. "Why not?"

"Because I'm not good father material."

At this, she looked aghast. Almost comically so. "Are you kidding me? You're incredible father material. You're smart and interesting and brave and funny and well traveled and smart and, holy cow, you're *gorgeous*."

He bit back a smile at that. "Thanks. But those aren't things that necessarily make a good father."

"Maybe not, but they make an *excellent* breeder."

* * *

Baby in the Making is part of the
Accidental Heirs series:

First they find their fortunes, then they find love

Dear Reader,

What's that old advice about writing? Write what you know? Well, I think it's safe to say I've rarely ascribed to that school of thought. So why start now?

In *Baby in the Making*, Yeager Novak is a major adventurer. Adventuring isn't just how he makes his living—it's how he lives his life. He's not happy unless he's standing on a literal precipice somewhere in the world, staring down death, with adrenaline pumping through his body. You know what makes adrenaline pump through *my* body? Spiders. Or seeing the gas gauge dip below a quarter of a tank. Or realizing I don't have a coupon for cat food this week.

Let's talk about something else, shall we?

Like how much more I have in common with Hannah Robinson, whose idea of adventure is taking the subway instead of the bus or using her pinking shears for cat-food coupons. When she discovers that she's not only New York's version of the missing Grand Duchess Anastasia, but that inheriting her long-lost family's fortune depends on her maternal potential, she knows she has to call in the big guns. And Yeager's guns are ridiculously big. She knows, because, as his seamstress, she's seen them dozens of times. Talk about adventure.

But neither of them is really ready for what's in store when it comes to creating life. Seriously, what greater adventure is there than parenthood? Unless maybe it's falling in love along the way.

I had so much fun writing about opposites-attract Hannah and Yeager. I hope you have fun reading about them, too.

Enjoy,

Elizabeth

ELIZABETH BEVARLY

—

BABY IN THE MAKING

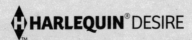

Recycling programs
for this product may
not exist in your area.

ISBN-13: 978-0-373-83889-9

Baby in the Making

Copyright © 2017 by Elizabeth Bevarly

All rights reserved. Except for use in any review, the reproduction or utilization of this work in whole or in part in any form by any electronic, mechanical or other means, now known or hereinafter invented, including xerography, photocopying and recording, or in any information storage or retrieval system, is forbidden without the written permission of the publisher, Harlequin Enterprises Limited, 225 Duncan Mill Road, Don Mills, Ontario M3B 3K9, Canada.

This is a work of fiction. Names, characters, places and incidents are either the product of the author's imagination or are used fictitiously, and any resemblance to actual persons, living or dead, business establishments, events or locales is entirely coincidental.

This edition published by arrangement with Harlequin Books S.A.

For questions and comments about the quality of this book, please contact us at CustomerService@Harlequin.com.

® and TM are trademarks of Harlequin Enterprises Limited or its corporate affiliates. Trademarks indicated with ® are registered in the United States Patent and Trademark Office, the Canadian Intellectual Property Office and in other countries.

Printed in U.S.A.

Elizabeth Bevarly is the award-winning, *New York Times* bestselling author of more than seventy books, novellas and screenplays. Although she has called home exotic places like San Juan, Puerto Rico and Haddonfield, New Jersey, she's now happily settled back in her native Kentucky with her husband and son. When she's not writing, she's binge-watching documentaries on Netflix, spending too much time on Reddit or making soup out of whatever she finds in the freezer. Visit her at elizabethbevarly.com for news about current and upcoming projects, for book, music and film recommendations, for recipes, and for lots of other fun stuff.

Books by Elizabeth Bevarly

Harlequin Desire

Taming the Prince
Taming the Beastly M.D.
Married to His Business
The Billionaire Gets His Way
My Fair Billionaire
Caught in the Billionaire's Embrace

Accidental Heirs

Only on His Terms
A CEO in Her Stocking
The Pregnancy Affair
A Beauty for the Billionaire
Baby in the Making

Visit her Author Profile page at Harlequin.com, or elizabethbevarly.com, for more titles.

For Eli,
My greatest creation ever.

Love you, Peanut.

One

Really, it wasn't the gaping hole in the shirt and pants that troubled Hannah Robinson most. It wasn't the bloodstain, either. She'd seen worse. No, what troubled her most was how little Yeager Novak seemed to be bothered by the six tidy stitches binding his flesh just north of the waistband of his silk boxers. Then again, as far as Yeager's garments were concerned, this was par for the course. Such was life sewing for a tailor whose most profitable client made his living at cheating death—and planning similar travel adventures for others—then brought in what was left of his clothing after the most recent near miss to have them mended. Or, in the case of the shirt, completely recreated from scratch.

Yeager towered over her from her current position kneeling before him, tape measure in hand. But then, he towered over her when she was standing, too. Shoving a handful of coal-black hair off his forehead, he gazed down at her with eyes the color of sapphires and said, "I'll never let a bull get that close to me again." He darted his gaze from the stitches on his torso to the ruined clothing on the floor. "That was just a little too close for comfort."

Hannah blew a dark blond curl out of her eyes and pushed her reading glasses higher on her nose. "That's what you said last year when you ran with the bulls."

He looked puzzled. "I did?"

"Yes. It was the first time you came to see us here at Cathcart and Quinn, because your previous tailor told you to take a hike when you brought in one too many of his masterpieces to be mended." She arched a brow in meaningful reminder. "Except when you were in Pamplona last July, you escaped into a cantina before the bull was able to do more than tear the leg of your trousers."

"Right," he said, remembering. "That was where I met Jimena. Who came back to my hotel with me while I changed my clothes. And didn't get back into them for hours." His expression turned sublime. "I probably should have sent that bull a thank-you note."

Even after knowing him for a year, Hannah was still sometimes surprised by the frankness with which Yeager talked about his sex life. Then again, his personal life sounded like it was almost as adventurous as his professional life, so maybe he had trouble distinguishing between the two on occasion.

"Or at least sent Jimena a text that said adios," Hannah said, striving for the same matter-of-factness and not sure if she quite managed it.

He grinned. "Hey, don't worry about Jimena. She got what she wanted, too."

I'll bet, Hannah thought, her gaze traveling to the elegant bumps of muscle and sinew on his torso. Yeager Novak might well have been sculpted by the hands of the gods. But the scar left behind by his latest stitches would be in good company, what with the jagged pink line marring the flesh above his navel and the puckered arc to their left. He had scars all over his body, thanks to his extreme adventurer ways. And thanks to his total lack of inhibition when it came to being fitted for clothes, Hannah had seen all of them.

"So you think you can fix the shirt and pants?" he asked.

"The pants will be fine," she told him. "They just need a good washing. But the shirt is a goner." Before he could open his mouth to protest, she added, "Don't worry, Mr. Novak. I can make a new one that will look just like it."

He threw her an exasperated look. "How many times have I told you to call me Yeager?"

"Lots," she replied. "And, just like I told you all those other times, it's Mr. Cathcart's and Mr. Quinn's policy to use 'Mr.' or 'Ms.' with all of our clients."

Just like it was Cathcart and Quinn policy that Hannah wear the ugly little smock she had to wear while working and always keep her hair confined, as if the shop's sole female employee was a throwback to the Industrial Revolution.

"Anyway," she continued, "I learned pretty quickly to keep all of your patterns and cut enough fabric for two garments whenever I make one."

He smiled in a way that was nothing short of devastating. "And I love you for it," he told her.

She smiled back. "I know."

Yeager told Hannah he loved her all the time. He loved her for making him clothes that fit like a glove. He loved her for mending them when he thought he'd ruined them. He loved her for being able to remove bloodstains, oil stains, pampas stains, baba ghanoush stains, walrus stains...stains from more sources than any normal human being saw in a lifetime. And, hey, she loved Yeager, too. The same way she loved cannoli and luna moths and sunsets—with a certain sense of awe that such things even existed in the world.

She went back to measuring his inseam, pretending the action commanded every scrap of her attention when, by now, she had Yeager's measurements memorized. There was no reason he had to know

that, was there? Sometimes a girl had to do what
a girl had to do. Especially when said girl was between boyfriends. Like eight months between boyfriends. None of whom had torsos roped with muscle
or smelled like a rugged, windswept canyon.

"Have you ever been to Spain, Hannah?" Yeager asked.

"I lived for a while in what used to be Spanish
Harlem," she told him as she penned his inseam mea-
surement onto the back of her hand. She lifted the
tape measure to his waist. "Does that count?"

He chuckled. "No. You should go to Spain. It's an
incredible country. Definitely in my top five favorite places to visit."

Hannah would have told him her top five were
Queens, Manhattan, Brooklyn, the Bronx and Staten
Island, since she'd never ventured outside the five
boroughs of New York. For fifteen of her first eighteen years, it was because she'd been a ward of the
state, and even though she'd been shuffled around *a
lot* during that time, she'd never landed outside the
city's jurisdiction. For the last nine years, she hadn't
had the funds to pay for something as frivolous as
travel. What didn't go to keeping herself housed and
fed went toward funding the business she'd started
out of her Sunnyside apartment. Things like travel
could wait until *after* she was the toast of the New
York fashion industry.

"What are your other top four favorite places?" she asked.

She was going to go out on a limb and say that, to a man who'd built a billion-dollar company out of creating extreme adventure vacations for other alpha types, Sunnyside and what used to be Spanish Harlem probably weren't going to make the cut.

He didn't even have to think about his response. "New Zealand, Slovenia, Chile and Iceland. But ask me tomorrow and it could be a whole different list."

Hannah jotted the last of his measurements onto the back of her hand with the others, returned the pen to its perennial place in the bun she always wore for work and stood. Yep, Yeager still towered over her. Then again, since she stood five-two, most people did.

"All done," she told him. Reluctantly she added, "You can get dressed now."

He nodded toward the clothes on the floor. "Thanks for taking care of this."

"No problem. But you know, you could save a lot of money on tailoring if you stayed in New York for more than a few weeks at a time."

"There's no way I can stay anywhere for more than a few weeks at a time," he said. "And I won't apologize for being an adventurer."

Hannah would never ask him to. She couldn't imagine Yeager sitting behind a desk punching a keyboard or standing on an assembly line screwing in machine parts. It would be like asking Superman to work as a parking attendant.

"All I'm saying is be careful."

He flinched. "Those are the last two words somebody like me wants to hear."

And they were the two words Hannah lived by. Not that she was a fearful person by any stretch of the imagination. You didn't survive a childhood and adolescence as a ward of the state by being timid. But after nearly a decade on her own, she'd carved out a life for herself that was quiet, steady and secure, and she was careful not to jeopardize that. Oh, blissful predictability. Oh, exalted stability. Oh, revered security. She'd never had any of those things growing up. No way would she risk losing them now.

"Your pants and new shirt will be ready a week from today," she told Yeager.

He thrust his arms through the sleeves of a gray linen shirt Hannah had made for him and began to button it. "Great. That'll be just in time for my trip to Gansbaai. South Africa," he clarified before she could ask. "I'm taking a group to go cage diving with great white sharks."

"Of course you are. Because after nearly being gored to death by a gigantic bull, why wouldn't you risk being bitten in two by a gigantic shark? It makes perfect sense."

He grinned again. "After that, it's off to Nunavut with a couple of buddies to climb Mount Thor."

"I would love to see your passport, Mr. Novak. It must be as thick as a novel."

"Yeah, it is. Like *Harry Potter and the Order of the Phoenix* size."

And the stories it could tell were probably every bit as fantastic.

"Well, have a good time," she told him. "I'll be at home, inventorying my swatches and organizing my bobbins."

He threw her one last smile as he reached for his charcoal trousers—also fashioned by Hannah. "And you say I live dangerously."

The bell above the shop entrance jingled, making her turn in that direction. "Excuse me," she said as she backed toward the fitting room entrance. "Your claim check will be at the register when you're ready."

The minute Hannah disappeared through the fitting room door, Yeager Novak's mind turned to other, more pressing, topics. When your life's work was creating extreme adventures for wealthy clients, you had to make plans, sometimes years in advance. In putting together vacation packages, he had a million things to consider—a country's culture and politics, its potential safety, its seasonal climate, how many people needed to be bribed for all the requisite permissions… The list was endless. And he always tried out the travel packages he designed for his clients first, to be sure they were doable without risk to life or limb.

Well, without *too* much risk to life or limb. *No* risk kind of defeated the purpose.

He knotted his tie, grabbed his suit jacket and headed for the register. Hannah's blond head was bent over her receipt pad as she wrote in her slow, precise hand, a few errant curls springing free of the prim little bun she always wore. Nice to know there was at least some part of her that wanted to break free of her buttoned-up, battened-down self. He'd never met anyone more straitlaced than Hannah… whatever her last name was.

As if she'd heard him say that out loud, she suddenly glanced up, her silver-gray eyes peering over the tops of her black half-glasses. She did have some beautiful eyes, though, he'd give her that. He'd never seen the color on another human being. But the rest of her… The shapeless jacket-thing she wore completely hid her gender, and if she was wearing any makeup, he sure couldn't see it. He guessed she was kind of cute in a wholesome, girl-next-door type of way, if you went for the wholesome, girl-next-door type—which he didn't. He liked talking to her, though. She was smart and funny. And, man, did her clothes make him look good. He knew nothing about sewing or fashion, but he knew excellent work when he saw it. And Hannah Whatshername definitely did excellent work.

"A week from today," she reiterated as she tore the receipt from the pad and extended it toward him.

"Thanks," he replied as he took it from her. "Any chance you could make a second shirt like it by then? Just in case?" Before she could object—because he could tell she was going to—he added, "There could be an extra hundred bucks in it for you."

She bit her lip thoughtfully, a gesture that was slightly—surprisingly—erotic. "I'm not allowed to take tips."

"Oh, c'mon. I don't see Leo or Monty around."

"Mr. Cathcart is on a buying trip to London," she said. "And Mr. Quinn is at lunch."

"Then they'll never know."

She expelled the kind of sigh someone makes when they know they're breaking the rules but they badly need cash for something. Yeager was intrigued. What could Ms. Goody Two-shoes Hannah need money for that would make her break the rules?

With clear reluctance she said, "I can't. I'm sorry. I just don't have time to do it here—we're so backlogged." Before he could protest, she hurried on. "However, I happen to know a seamstress who does freelance work at home. She's very good."

Yeager shook his head. "No way. I don't trust anyone with my clothes but you."

"No, you don't understand, Mr. Novak. I guarantee you'll like this woman's work. I know her *intimately*."

"But—"

"You could even say that she and I are *one of a kind*. If you know what I mean."

She eyed him pointedly. And after a moment, Yeager understood. Hannah was the one who did freelance work at home. "Gotcha."

"If you happened to do a search on Craigslist for, say, 'Sunnyside seamstress,' she'd be the first listing that pops up. Ask if she can make you a shirt by next week for the same price you'd pay here, and I guarantee she'll be able to do it."

Yeager grabbed his phone from his pocket and pulled up Craigslist. He should have known Hannah would live in Sunnyside. It was the closest thing New York had to Small Town America.

"Found you," he said.

She frowned at him.

"I mean…found *her*."

"Send her an email from that listing. I'm sure she'll reply when she gets home from work tonight."

He was already typing when he said, "Great. Thanks."

"But you'll have to pick it up at my—I mean, her place," she told him. "She can't bring it here, and she doesn't deliver."

"No problem."

He sent the email then returned his phone to one pocket as he tugged his wallet from another. He withdrew five twenties from the ten he always had on him and placed them on the counter. Hannah's eyes widened at the gesture, but she discreetly palmed the bills and tucked them into her pocket.

Even so, she asked, "Don't you want to wait until you have the extra shirt?"

He shook his head. "I trust you."

"Thanks."

"No, thank *you*. That was my favorite shirt. It will be nice to have a spare. Not that I'll be letting any sharks near my clothes, but you never know when you'll meet another Jimena."

She nodded, but he was pretty sure it wasn't in understanding. Someone like her probably wouldn't let a lover that spontaneous and temporary get anywhere near her. She was way too buttoned-up, battened-down and straitlaced for idle encounters, regardless of how beautiful her eyes were or how erotically she bit her lip. Hannah, he was certain, only dated the same kind of upright, forthright, do-right person she was. To Yeager, that would be a fate worse than death.

"I'll see you in a week," he said, lifting a hand in farewell.

As he made his way to the door, he heard her call after him, "Have a great day, Mr. Novak! And remember to look both ways before you cross the street!"

A week later—the day Yeager was scheduled to pick up his new shirt at her apartment, in fact—

Hannah was in the back room of Cathcart and Quinn, collecting fabric remnants to take home with her. Everyone else had gone for the day, and she was counting the minutes until she could begin closing up shop, when the store's entrance bell rang to announce a customer. Hoping it would just be someone picking up an alteration, she headed out front.

She didn't recognize the man at the register, but he had the potential to become a client, judging by his bespoke suit from… Aponte's, she decided. It looked like Paolo's work. The man's blond hair was cut with razor-precision, his eyes were cool and keen, and his smile was this just side of dispassionate.

"Hello," Hannah greeted him as she approached. "May I help you?"

"Hannah Robinson?" he asked. Her surprise that he knew her must have been obvious, because he quickly added, "My name is Gus Fiver. I'm an attorney with Tarrant, Fiver and Twigg. We're a probate law firm here in Manhattan."

His response only surprised her more. She didn't have a will herself, and she knew no one who might have included her in one. Her lack of connections was what had landed her in the foster care system as a three-year-old, after her mother died with no surviving relatives or friends to care for her. And although Hannah hadn't had any especially horrible experiences in the system, she could safely say she'd never met anyone there who would remember her in their last wishes. There was no reason a probate attorney should know her name or where she worked.

"Yes," she said cautiously. "I'm Hannah Robinson."

Gus Fiver's smile grew more genuine at her response. In a matter of seconds he went from being a high-powered Manhattan attorney to an affable boy next door. The change made Hannah feel a little better.

"Excellent," he said. Even his voice was warmer now.

"I'm sorry, but how do you know me?" she asked.

"My firm has been looking for you since the beginning of the year. And one of our clients was looking for you long before then."

"I don't understand. Why would anyone be looking for me? Especially when I'm not that hard to find?"

Instead of answering her directly he said, "You did most of your growing up in the foster care system, yes?"

Hannah was so stunned he would know that about her—few of her friends even knew—that she could only nod.

"You entered the program when you were three, I believe, after your mother, Mary Robinson, died."

Her stomach knotted at the realization that he would know about her past so precisely. But she automatically replied, "Yes."

"And do you remember what your life was like prior to that?"

"Mr. Fiver, what's this about?"

Instead of explaining he said, "Please, just bear with me for a moment, Ms. Robinson."

Hannah didn't normally share herself with other people until she'd known them for some time, and even then, there were barriers it took a while for most people to breach. But there was something about Gus Fiver that told her it was okay to trust him. To a point.

So she told him, "I only have a few vague memories. I know my mother was a bookkeeper for a welding company on Staten Island and that that's where she and I were living when she died. But I only know that because that's what I've been told. I don't have any mementos or anything. Everything she owned was sold after her death, and what was left in her estate after it was settled was put into trust for me until I turned eighteen and was booted out of the system."

Not that there had been much, but it had allowed Hannah to start life on her own without a lot of the stress she would have had otherwise, and she'd been enormously grateful for it.

"Is your mother the one you inherited your eyes from?" Mr. Fiver asked. "I don't mean to be forward, but they're such an unusual color."

Hannah had fielded enough remarks about her singularly colored eyes—even from total strangers—

that she no longer considered them forward. "No," she said. "My mother had blue eyes."

"So you at least remember what she looked like?"

Hannah shook her head. "No. But I take back what I said about mementos. I do have one. A photograph of my mother that one of the social workers was kind enough to frame and give to me before I went into the system. Somehow, I always managed to keep it with me whenever they moved me to a new place."

This interested Mr. Fiver a lot. "Is there any chance you have this photograph with you?"

"I do, actually." Hannah had taken it out of the frame when she was old enough to have a wallet, because she'd always wanted to carry the photo with her. It was the only evidence of her mother she'd ever had.

"May I see it?" Mr. Fiver asked.

Hannah was about to tell him no, that this had gone on long enough. But her damnable curiosity now had the better of her, and she was kind of interested to see where this was going.

"It's in my wallet," she said.

He smiled again, notching another chink in her armor that weakened her mettle. "I don't mind waiting."

She retrieved her purse from beneath the counter and withdrew the photo, now creased and battered, from its plastic sheath to hand to Mr. Fiver. It had been cropped from what must have been a studio portrait, and showed her mother from the chest up, along with the shoulder of someone sitting next to her.

"And your father?" he asked as he studied the picture.

"I didn't know him," Hannah said. "He's listed as a Robert Williams on my birth certificate, but do you know how many Robert Williamses there are in New York alone? No one ever found him. I never had any family but my mother."

Mr. Fiver returned the photo to her. "The reason we've been looking for you, Ms. Robinson, is because we have a client whose estate we've been managing since his death while we search for his next of kin. That's sort of our specialty at Tarrant, Fiver and Twigg. We locate heirs whose whereabouts or identities are unknown. We believe you may be this client's sole heir."

"I'm sorry to disappoint you, Mr. Fiver, but that's impossible. If my mother had had any family, the state would have found them twenty-five years ago."

He opened his portfolio and sifted through its contents, finally withdrawing an eight-by-ten photo he held up for Hannah to see. It was the same picture of her mother she had been carrying her entire life, but it included the person who'd been cropped from her copy—a man with blond hair and silver-gray eyes. Even more startling, a baby with the exact same coloring was sitting in her mother's lap.

Her gaze flew to Mr. Fiver's. But she had no idea what to say.

"This is a photograph of Stephen and Alicia Linden of Scarsdale, New York," he said. "The baby is their daughter, Amanda. Mrs. Linden and Amanda disappeared not long after this picture was taken."

A strange buzzing erupted in Hannah's head. How could Gus Fiver have a photo of her mother identical to hers? Was the baby in her mother's lap Hannah? Was the man her father? What the hell was going on?

All she could say, though, was, "I don't understand."

"One day, while Stephen Linden was at work in the city," Mr. Fiver continued, "Alicia bundled up ten-month-old Amanda and, with nothing but the clothes on their backs, left him." He paused for a moment, as if he were trying to choose his next words carefully. "Stephen Linden was, from all accounts, a…difficult man to live with. He…mistreated his wife. Badly. Alicia feared for her and her daughter's safety, but her husband's family was a very powerful one and she worried they would hinder her in her efforts to leave him. So she turned to an underground group active in aiding battered women, providing them with new identities and forged documents and small amounts of cash. With the assistance of this group, Alicia and Amanda Linden of Scarsdale were able to start a new life as Mary and Hannah Robinson of Staten Island."

By now, Hannah was reeling. She heard what Mr. Fiver was saying, but none of it quite registered. "I… I'm sorry, Mr. Fiver, but this… You're telling me I'm not the person I've always thought I was? That my whole life should have been different from the one I've lived? That's just… It's…"

Then another thought struck her and the air rushed from her lungs in a quick whoosh. Very softly, she asked, "Is my father still alive?"

At this, Mr. Fiver sobered. "No, I'm sorry. He died almost twenty years ago. Our client, who initially launched the search for you, was your paternal grandfather." He paused a telling beat before concluding, "Chandler Linden."

Had there been any breath left in Hannah, she would have gasped. Everyone in New York knew the name Chandler Linden. His ancestors had practically built this city, and, at the time of his death, he'd still owned a huge chunk of it.

Although she had no idea how she managed it, Hannah said, "Chandler Linden was a billionaire."

Mr. Fiver nodded. "Yes, he was. Ms. Robinson, you might want to close up shop early today. You and I have *a lot* to talk about."

Two

Yeager Novak didn't find himself in Queens very often. Or, for that matter, ever. And he wasn't supposed to be here now. His assistant, Amira, was supposed to be picking up his shirt at Hannah's. But she'd needed to take the afternoon off for a family emergency, so he'd told her he would deal with whatever was left on his agenda today himself—not realizing at the time that that would include going to Queens. By train. Which was another place he didn't find himself very often. Or, for that matter, ever. This time of day, though, the train was fastest and easiest, and he needed to be back in Manhattan ASAP.

But as he walked down Greenpoint Avenue toward 44th Street, he couldn't quite make himself

hurry. Queens was different from Manhattan—
less frantic, more relaxed. Especially now, at the
end of the workday. The sun was hanging low in
the sky, bathing the stunted brick buildings in gold
and amber. Employees in storefronts were turning
over Closed signs as waiters at cafés unfolded sand-
wich boards with nightly specials scrawled in bright-
colored chalk. People on the street actually smiled
and said hello to him as he passed. With every step
he took, Yeager felt like he was moving backward in
time, and somehow, that made him want to go slower.
Hannah's neighborhood was even more quaint than
he'd imagined.

He hated quaint. At least, he usually did. Somehow the quaintness of Sunnyside was less off-putting
than most.

Whatever. To each his own. Yeager would suffocate in a place like this. Quiet. Cozy. Family friendly.
Why was a healthy, red-blooded young woman with
beautiful silver-gray eyes and a surprisingly erotic
lip nibble living somewhere like this? Not that anything Hannah did was Yeager's business. But he did
kind of wonder.

Her apartment was on the third and uppermost
floor of one of those tawny brick buildings, above
a Guatemalan *mercado*. He rang her bell and identified himself, and she buzzed him in. At the top of
the stairs were three apartments. Hannah had said

hers was B, but before he even knocked on the door, she opened it.

At least, he thought it was Hannah who opened it. She didn't look much like the woman he knew from Cathcart and Quinn. The little black half-glasses were gone and the normally bunned-up hair danced around her shoulders in loose, dark gold curls. In place of her shapeless work jacket, she had on a pair of striped shorts and a sleeveless red shirt knotted at her waist. As small as she was, she had surprisingly long legs and they ended in feet whose toenails were an even brighter red than her shirt.

But what really made him think someone else had taken Hannah's place was her expression. He'd never seen her be anything but cool and collected. This version looked agitated and anxious.

"Hannah?" he asked, just to be sure.

"Yeah, hi," she said. She sounded even more on edge than she looked. "I'm sorry. I totally forgot about your pickup tonight."

"Didn't my assistant email you yesterday to confirm?"

"She did, actually. But today was…" She shook her head as if trying to physically clear it of something. But that didn't seem to work, because she still looked distracted. "I got some, um, very weird news today. But it's okay, your shirt is finished." She hurried on. "I just…" She inhaled a deep breath, released it in a ragged sigh…and still looked as if she were a million miles away. "I forgot about the pickup," she said again. Almost as an afterthought, she added, "Come on in."

She opened the door wider and stepped back to get out of his way. Good thing, too, since the room he walked into was actually an alcove that was barely big enough to hold both of them. As he moved forward, Hannah wedged herself behind him to close the door, brushing against him—with all that naked skin—as she did. It was then he noticed something about her he'd never noticed before. She smelled like raspberries. Really ripe, really succulent, raspberries.

Another step forward took him into her apartment proper, but it wasn't much bigger than the alcove and seemed to consist of only one room. Yeager looked for doors that would lead to others, but saw only one, which had to be for the bathroom. The "kitchen" was a couple of appliances tucked into another alcove adjacent to the single window in the place, one that offered a view of a building on the next street. The apartment was furnished with the bare essentials for living and the tools of a seamstress's trade—a sewing machine and ironing board, a trio of torso stands for works-in-progress, stacks of fabric and a rack of plastic-covered garments.

"I guess my place is a little smaller than yours, huh?" Hannah asked, obviously sensing his thoughts.

Smaller than his *place*? Her apartment was smaller than his bedroom. But all he said was, "A bit."

She squeezed out of the alcove, past him—leaving that tantalizing scent of raspberries in her wake—and strode to the rolling rack, from which she withdrew one of the plastic-covered garments. As he followed, he noted a half-empty bottle of wine on one of the end tables by the love seat. He thought maybe he'd interrupted a romantic evening she was spending with someone else—the bathroom door was closed—then noted that the near-empty glass sitting behind the bottle was alone.

"Do you want to try it on before you take it?" she asked. "Just to be sure it fits?"

Yeager figured it probably wasn't a bad idea, since he was leaving in two days for South Africa and there wouldn't be time for Amira to come back for it if it needed alterations. Truth be told, he also wasn't sure he should leave Hannah alone just yet, what with the wine, the distraction and the anxious look…and, okay, all that naked skin.

"Yeah, I guess I should, just in case," he replied.

As she removed the plastic from the shirt, he tossed his suit jacket onto the love seat, tugged free his tie and unbuttoned the shirt he was wearing. By the time he shed it, she was holding up his new one for him to slip on. She looked a little steadier now and seemed more like herself. His concern began to ease a bit. Until he drew near and saw that her eyes housed a healthy bit of panic.

It was obvious there was something bothering her.

A lot. Yeager told himself that whatever it was, it was none of his business. But that didn't keep him from wondering. Boyfriend troubles? Family conflicts? Problems at work? He knew nothing about her outside her job. Because there was no reason for him to know anything about her outside her job. There was no reason for him to care, either. That wasn't to be cold or unfeeling. That was just how he was. He didn't care about much of anything outside his immediate sphere of existence. Somehow, though, he suddenly kind of cared about Hannah.

"I'm sorry," she said as he thrust his arm through the shirt's sleeve, "but the fabric isn't exactly the same as the original. Since I was moonlighting, I couldn't use what we have at work, and that came from Portugal. But I found a beautiful dobby in nearly the same color. I hope it's okay. It brought the price down a bit."

Yeager couldn't have cared less about the price. He cared about quality and style. Maybe it was superficial, but a man who was the face of a Fortune 500 company had to look good. And, thanks to Hannah, he always did.

"No, this is good," he said. "It's got a great texture. I actually like this one better than the one you made for me at Cathcart and Quinn. Why aren't you the one they're sending on buying trips to London and Portugal?"

"You'll have to ask Mr. Cathcart that question,"

she said in a way that made him think she'd already broached the topic with her employer and been shot down. Probably more than once.

"Maybe I will," he said, wondering about his sudden desire to act as her champion. "Or maybe you should just open your own business."

As she studied the fit of his shirt, she gestured to the rack of clothes against the wall. "I'm trying."

Out of curiosity, Yeager walked over to look at what she'd made for her other clients. He was surprised to see that the majority of items hanging there were children's clothes.

"You mostly make stuff for kids?" he asked.

Instead of replying, Hannah moved to her sewing machine to withdraw a business card from a stack and handed it to Yeager. It was pale lavender, imprinted with the words, Joey & Kit, and decorated with a logo of a kangaroo and fox touching noses. Below them was the slogan, "Glad rags for happy kids." At the bottom were addresses for a website, an email and a PO box.

"This is your business?" Yeager asked, holding up the card.

She nodded. "I'm an S-corporation. I trademarked the name and logo and everything."

"Why kids' clothes? Seems like other areas of fashion would be more profitable."

"They would be," she said. He waited for her to elaborate. She didn't. He was about to ask her to when she told him, "Turn around, so I can make sure the back darts are aligned."

He did as she instructed, something that left him looking out the apartment's solitary window. He didn't know why, but it really bothered him that Hannah only had one window from which to view the world. His West Chelsea penthouse had panoramic views of Manhattan and the Hudson from floor-to-ceiling windows in most rooms—including two of the three-and-a-half baths. Not that he spent much time at home, but his office in the Flatiron District had pretty breathtaking views of the city, too. No matter where Yeager went in the world, he always made sure he had a lot to look at. Mountain ranges that disappeared into clouds, savannas that dissolved into the horizon, oceans that met the stars in the distant night sky. Some of the best parts of adventure travel were just looking at things. But Hannah lived her life in a square little room with one window that opened onto a building across the way.

"You know, I don't usually have to put darts in a man's shirt," she said. "But the way you're built… broad shoulders, tapered waist…"

Yeager told himself he only imagined the sigh of approval he heard.

"Anyway," she went on, "I think this looks good."

She ran her hand down the length of his back on one side, then up again on the other, smoothing out the seams in question. The gesture was in no way protracted or flirtatious. Her touch was deft and professional. Yet, somehow, it made his pulse twitch.

She stepped in front of him, gave him a final once-over with eyes that still looked a little haunted, and told him, "You're good to go."

It was one of his favorite statements to hear. Yeager loved going. Anywhere. Everywhere. Whenever he could. Strangely, though, in that moment, he didn't want to go. He told himself it was because, in spite of the relative ease of the last few minutes, there was still something about Hannah that was... off. He'd never seen her be anything but upbeat. This evening, she was subdued. And that just didn't sit well with him.

Before he realized what he was doing, he asked, "Hannah, is everything okay?"

Her eyes widened in now unmistakable panic. She opened her mouth to reply but no words emerged. Which may have been his biggest tip-off yet that there was something seriously wrong. Hannah was never at a loss for words. On the contrary, she was generally one of those people who had a snappy reply for everything.

He tried again. "You just don't seem like yourself tonight."

For a moment she looked as if she was going to deny anything was wrong. Then she made a defeated sound and her whole body seemed to slump forward.

"Is this about the weird news you got today?" he asked.

She nodded, but instead of looking at him, she lowered her gaze to the floor. Hannah never did that. She was one of the most direct people he knew, always making eye contact. It was one of the things he loved about her. So few people did that.

"What kind of news was it?"

She hesitated again, still not looking at him. Finally she said, "The kind that could not only completely change my future, but also confirmed that my past could have—should have—been a lot better than it was."

"I'm not sure I understand."

At this, she emitted a strangled chuckle completely devoid of humor. "Yeah, I know the feeling."

Maybe the wine had affected her more than he thought. Probably, he ought to just drop it and pay her for his shirt. Definitely, he should be getting the hell out of there.

Instead he heard himself ask, "Do you want to talk about it?"

At that, she finally pulled her gaze from the floor and met his squarely...for all of a nanosecond. Then she lifted both hands to cover her beautiful silver-gray eyes. Then her lips began to tremble. Then she sniffled. Twice. And that was when Yeager knew he was in trouble. Because Hannah crying was way worse than Hannah panicking. Panic eventually subsided. But sadness… Sadness could go on forever. No one knew that better than he did.

She didn't start crying, though. Not really. After a moment she wiped both eyes with the backs of her hands and dropped them to hug herself tight. But that gesture just made her look even more lost. Especially since her eyes were still damp. Something in Yeager's chest twisted tight at seeing her this way. He had no idea why. He barely knew her. He just hated seeing anyone this distraught.

"Holy crap, do I want to talk about it," she said softly. "I just don't have anyone to talk about it with."

That should have been his cue to get out while he still had the chance. The last thing he had time for—hell, the last thing he wanted—was to listen to someone whose last name he didn't even know talk about her life-altering problems. He should be heading for the front door stat. And he would. Any minute now. Any second now. In five, four, three, two…

"Give me one minute to change my shirt," he told her, wondering what the hell had possessed him. "Then you can tell me about it."

While Yeager changed his shirt, Hannah moved to the love seat, perching herself on the very edge of the cushion and wondering what just happened. One minute, she'd been double-checking the fit of his shirt and had been almost—*almost*—able to forget, if only for a moment, everything she'd learned today from Gus Fiver. The next minute, Yeager had been offering a sympathetic shoulder to cry on.

Not that she would cry on him. Well, probably not. She didn't want to ruin his shirt. But she appreciated his offer to hang around for a little while. She hadn't felt more alone in her life than she had over the last few hours.

She'd taken Gus Fiver's advice to close Cathcart and Quinn early, then had sat with him in the empty shop for nearly an hour as he'd given her all the specifics about her situation. A situation that included the most stunning good news/bad news scenario she'd ever heard. Since then she'd been here in her apartment, combing the internet for information about her newly discovered family and mulling everything she'd learned, in the hope that it would help her make sense of the choice she had to make. Maybe someone like Yeager, who didn't have any personal involvement, would have a clearer perspective and some decent advice.

She watched as he changed his shirt, doing her best not to stare at the cords of muscle and sinew roping his arms, shoulders and torso. But in an apartment the size of hers, there wasn't much else to stare at. Then again, even if she'd had the frescoes of the Sistine Chapel surrounding her, it would still be Yeager that drew her eye. So she busied herself with filling her wineglass a third time, since the two glasses she'd already consumed had done nothing to take the edge off.

"You want a glass of wine?" she asked Yeager, belatedly realizing how negligent a hostess she'd been.

Also belatedly, she remembered she'd picked up the wine at Duane Reade on her way home from work. She reread the label as she placed it back on the table. Chateau Yvette claimed to be a "wine product" that paired well with pizza and beef stew. It probably wasn't a brand Yeager normally bought for himself. But it was too late to retract the offer now.

"Yeah, that'd be great," he said as he finished buttoning his shirt.

She retrieved another glass from the kitchen and poured the wine. By then, Yeager had draped the plastic back over his new shirt and was sitting on the love seat—taking up most of it. So much so that his thigh aligned with hers when she sat and handed him his glass. She enjoyed another healthy swig from her own and grimaced. She honestly hadn't realized until then how, uh, not-particularly-good it was. Probably because her head had been too full of *Omigod, omigod, omigod, what am I going to do?*

"So what's up?" he asked.

She inhaled a deep breath and released it slowly. It still came out shaky and uneven. Not surprising, since shaky and uneven was how she'd been feeling since Gus Fiver had dropped his Chandler Linden bombshell. There was nothing like the prospect of inheriting billions of dollars to send a person's pulse and brain synapses into overdrive.

If Hannah actually inherited it.

She took another breath and this time when she released it, it was a little less ragged. "Have you heard of a law firm called Tarrant, Fiver and Twigg?" she asked.

Yeager nodded. "Yeah. They're pretty high-profile. A lot of old money—big money—clients."

"Well, I had a meeting with one of their partners this afternoon."

Yeager couldn't quite hide his surprise that someone like her would be in touch with such a financial powerhouse, though he was obviously trying to. Hannah appreciated his attempt to be polite, but it was unnecessary. She wasn't bothered by being working class, nor was she ashamed of her upbringing. Even if she didn't talk freely about her past, she'd never tried to hide it, and she wasn't apologetic about the way she lived now. She'd done pretty well for herself and lived the best life she could. She was proud of that.

Still, she replied, "I know. They're not exactly my social stratum. But I didn't contact them. They contacted me."

"About?" he asked.

"About the fact that I'm apparently New York's equivalent to the Grand Duchess Anastasia of Russia."

Now Yeager looked puzzled. So she did her best

to explain. Except she ended up not so much explaining as just pouring out her guts into his lap.

Without naming names, and glossing over many of the details, she told him about her discovery that she'd been born to a family she never knew she had in a town she would have sworn she'd never visited. She told him about her father's addiction and abuse and about her mother's custodial kidnapping of her. She told him about their false identities and their move from Scarsdale to Staten Island. She told him about her mother's death when she was three and her entry into the foster care system, where she'd spent the next fifteen years. And she told him about how, in a matter of minutes today, she went from living the ordinary life of a seamstress to becoming one of those long-lost heirs to a fortune who seemed only to exist in over-the-top fiction.

Through it all, Yeager said not a word. When she finally paused—not that she was finished talking by a long shot, because there was still *so much more* to tell him—he only studied her in silence. Then he lifted the glass of wine he had been holding through her entire story and, in one long quaff, drained it.

And then he grimaced, too. Hard. "That," he finally said, "was unbelievable."

"I know," Hannah told him. "But it's all true."

He shook his head. "No, I mean the wine. It was unbelievably bad."

"Oh."

"Your life is… Wow."

For a moment he only looked out at her little apartment without speaking. Then he looked at Hannah again.

And he said, "This isn't the kind of conversation to be having over unbelievably bad wine."

"It isn't?"

He shook his head. "No. This is the kind of conversation that needs to be had over extremely good Scotch."

"I don't have any Scotch." And even if she did, it wouldn't be extremely good.

He roused a smile. "Then we'll just have to go find some, won't we?"

Three

Instead of extremely good Scotch, they found a sufficiently good Irish whiskey at a pub up the street from Hannah's apartment. She'd ducked into the bathroom to change before they'd left, trading her shorts for a printed skirt that matched her shirt and dipping her feet into a pair of flat sandals. By the time the bartender brought their drinks to them at a two-seater cocktail table tucked into the corner of the dimly lit bar, she was beginning to feel a little more like herself.

Until she looked at Yeager and found him eyeing her with a scrutiny unlike any she'd ever had from him before. Normally he showed her no more interest than he would…well, a seamstress who was sewing some clothes for him. Sure, the two of them bantered back and forth whenever he was in the shop, but it was the kind of exchange everybody shared with people they saw in passing on any given day—baristas, cashiers, doormen, that kind of thing. In the shop, his attention passed with the moments. But now...

Now, Yeager Novak's undivided attention was an awesome thing. His sapphire eyes glinted like the gems they resembled, and if she'd fancied he could see straight into her soul before, now she was certain of it. Her heart began to hammer hard in her chest, her blood began to zip through her veins and her breathing became more shallow than it had been all day. This time, though, the reactions had little to do with the news of her massive potential inheritance and a lot to do with Yeager.

He must have sensed her reaction—hyperventilation was generally a dead giveaway—because he nudged her glass closer to her hand and said, "Take a couple sips of your drink. Then tell me again about how you ended up in Staten Island."

She wanted to start talking now, but she did as he instructed and enjoyed a few slow sips of her whiskey. She wasn't much of a drinker, usually sticking to wine or some sissy, fruit-sprouting drink. The liquor was smooth going down, warming her mouth and throat and chest. She closed her eyes to let it do its thing, then opened them again to find Yeager still studying her. She was grateful for the dim lighting of the bar. Not just because it helped soothe her rattled nerves but because it might mask the effect he was having on her.

"According to Mr. Fiver," she said, "my mother got help from a group of women who aided other women in escaping their abusers. They paid counterfeiters to forge new identities for both of us—fake social security numbers, fake birth certificates, the works. I don't know how my mother found them, but she needed them because my father's family was super powerful and probably could have kept her from leaving him or, at least, made sure she couldn't take me with her."

"And just who was your father's family?"

Hannah hesitated. During her internet search of her birth name, she had come across a number of items about her and her mother's disappearance from Scarsdale a quarter century ago. Some of them had been articles that appeared in newspapers and magazines shortly after the fact, but many of them were fairly current on "unsolved mystery" type blogs and websites. It had been singularly creepy to read posts about herself from strangers speculating on her fate. Some people were convinced Stephen Linden had beaten his wife and daughter to death and disposed of their bodies, getting away with murder, thanks to his social standing. Some thought baby Amanda had been kidnapped by strangers for ransom and that her mother had interrupted the crime and been killed by the perpetrators, her body dumped in Long Island Sound. Other guesses were closer to the truth: that Alicia escaped her abusive marriage with Amanda in tow and both were living now in the safety of a foreign country.

What would Yeager make of all this?

Since Hannah had already told him so much—and still had a lot more to reveal—she said, "My father's name was Stephen Linden. He died about twenty years ago. It was my recently deceased grandfather, Chandler Linden, who was looking for me and wanted to leave me the family fortune."

Yeager studied her in silence for a moment. Then he said, "You're Amanda Linden."

She had thought he would remark on her grandfather's identity, not hers. But she guessed she shouldn't be surprised by his knowing about Amanda's disappearance, too, since so many others did.

"You know about that," she said.

He chuckled. "Hannah, everyone knows about that. Any kid who was ever curious about unsolved crimes has read about the disappearance of Amanda Linden and her mother." He lifted a shoulder and let it drop. "When I was in middle school, I wanted to be a private investigator. I was totally into that stuff."

"Yeah, well, I wasn't," she said. "I had no idea any of this happened. Let alone that it happened to me."

She took another sip of her drink and was surprised by how much she liked the taste. Since Yeager had ordered it, it was doubtless the best this place had. Maybe her Linden genes just had a natural affinity for the finer things in life. She sipped her drink again.

"So you were destined for a life of wealth and privilege," Yeager said, "and instead, you grew up in the New York foster care system."

"Yep."

"And how was that experience?"

Hannah dropped her gaze to her drink, dragging her finger up and down the side of the glass. "It wasn't as terrible as what some kids go through," she said. "But it wasn't terrific, either. I mean a couple of times I landed in a really good place, with really good people. But just when I started to think maybe I'd found a spot where I fit in and could be reasonably happy for a while, I always got yanked out and put somewhere else where I didn't fit in and wasn't particularly happy."

She glanced up to find that he was looking at her as if she were some interesting specimen under a microscope. A specimen he couldn't quite figure out. So she returned her attention to her glass.

"That was the worst part, you know?" she continued. "Never feeling like I belonged anywhere. Never feeling like I had a real home or a real family. Now I know that I could have and should have—that I actually *did* have—both. The irony is that if I'd grown up as Amanda Linden, with all her wealth and privilege, I would have had a terrifying father who beat up my mother and very well could have come after me. Foster care was no picnic, but I was never physically abused. Dismissed and belittled, yeah. Neglected, sure. But never harmed. As Amanda, though…"

She didn't finish the statement. She didn't dare. She didn't even want to think about what kind of life she might have lived if her mother hadn't rescued her from it. What kind of life her mother had endured for years before her daughter's safety had compelled her to run.

"Some people would argue that neglect and belittlement *are* harm," Yeager said softly.

"Maybe," she conceded. "But I'd rather be neglected and belittled and shuffled around and have nothing to my name than live in the lap of luxury and go through what my mother must have gone through to make her escape the way she did. I just wish she'd had more time to enjoy her life once she got it back."

And Hannah wished she'd had more time herself to get to know her mother. Mary Robinson, formerly Alicia Linden, might very well have saved her daughter's life—both figuratively and literally. Yet Hannah had no way to thank her.

"Your grandfather, Chandler Linden, was a billionaire," Yeager said in the same matter-of-fact tone he'd been using all night.

Hannah's stomach pitched to have the knowledge

she'd been carrying around in her head all evening spoken aloud. Somehow, having it out in the open like that made it so much more real. Her heart began to thunder again and her vision began to swim. Hyperventilation would come next, so she enjoyed another, larger, taste of her drink in an effort to stave it off.

"Yeah," she said quietly when she set her glass on the table. "He was."

"Which means that now you're a billionaire," Yeager said in the same casual tone.

Oh, boy. There went her stomach again. "Well, I *could* be a billionaire," she told him.

"*Could* be?" he echoed. "You said your grandfather bequeathed his entire estate to you. What are they waiting on? A DNA test?"

"Mr. Fiver took a sample of my saliva while we were talking," she said. "But that's just a formality for the courts. There's no question I'm Amanda. I didn't just inherit my father's unique eye color. I also have a crescent-shaped birthmark on my right shoulder blade that shows up with some regularity in the Linden line. And, yes, my grandfather wants his entire estate to go to me. But there are certain… terms…of his will that need to be met before I can inherit."

"What kind of terms?"

Hannah threw back the rest of her drink in one long gulp. Before her glass even hit the table, Yeager was lifting a hand to alert the bartender that they wanted another round. He even pointed at Hannah and added, "Make hers a double."

Hannah started to tell him that wouldn't be necessary. Then she remembered her grandfather's demands again and grabbed Yeager's drink, downing what was left of it, too. She would need all the false courage she could get if she was going to actually talk about this. Especially with someone like Yeager.

Once the whiskey settled in her stomach—woo, that warmth was starting to feel really good—she did her best to gather her thoughts, even though they all suddenly wanted to go wandering off in different directions. And she did her best to explain.

"Okay, so, as rich as the Lindens have always been," she said, "they weren't particularly, um, fruitful. I'm the last of the line. My father was an only child, and he didn't remarry before his death. My grandfather's sister never married or had children. Their father had twin brothers, but they both died from influenza before they were even teenagers. The Linden family tree prior to that had been growing sparser and sparser with each ensuing generation, so I'm all that's left of them."

Her thoughts were starting to get a little fuzzy, so Hannah drew in another long breath and let it go. There. That was better. Kind of. Where was she? Besides about to have a panic attack? Oh, right. The dried-up Linden family tree.

"*Any*way…" She started again. "I guess my grandfather was sort of horrified by the idea that the world
would no longer be graced with the Linden family
presence—we were, I have learned, some of the best
fat cats and exploiters of the proletariat out there—so
he tied some strings to my inheritance."

"What kind of strings?" Yeager asked.

"Well, actually it's only one string," she told him.
"A string that's more like a rope. A rope that's tied
into a noose."

He was starting to look confused. She felt his
pain.

"Hannah, I think I can safely say that I have no
idea what you're talking about."

She tried again. "My grandfather included a condition I'll have to meet before I can inherit the family
fortune. He wanted to make sure that I, um, further
the Linden line."

"Further the line?"

She nodded. Then nodded some more. And then
some more. Why couldn't she stop nodding? And
why did her head feel like it was beginning to discon-
nect from her body? With great effort, she stilled and
tried to think of the most tactful way to tell Yeager
how her grandfather had stipulated that, before she
could inherit the piles and piles and *piles* of Linden
moolah, she'd have to become a Linden baby factory.

Finally she decided on, "My grandfather has stipulated that, before I can inherit the piles and piles

and *piles* of Linden moolah, I have to become a Linden baby factory."

Yeager's eyebrows shot up to nearly his hairline. "He wants you to procreate in order to inherit?"

Yeah, that would have been a much more tactful way to say it. Oh, well. "That's exactly what he wants," she said. "It's what he demands. In order to inherit the family fortune, I have to either already be a mother or on my way to becoming one."

"Can he do that?"

"Apparently so. The wording of his will was something along the lines of, if, when I was located after his death, I had a child or children, then no problem, here's more money than you could have ever imagined having, don't spend it all in one place."

"But you don't have a child or children," Yeager pointed out.

"Nope."

"So what happens in that case?"

"In that case, I have six months to get pregnant."

Yeager's eyebrows shot back up. "And what happens if you don't get pregnant in six months?"

"Then *aaaallllll* the Linden money will go to charity and I'll get a small severance package of fifty grand for my troubles, thanks so much for playing. Which, don't get me wrong, would be great, and I'd be most appreciative, but…"

"It's not billions."

"Right."

He opened his mouth to say something then closed it again. For another moment he studied her in silence. Then he said, "Well, that sucks."

"Yeah."

The bartender arrived with their drinks and Hannah immediately enjoyed a healthy swallow of hers.

"See, though," she said afterward, "the problem isn't with me having children. I've always planned on having kids someday. I want to have kids. I love kids. I wouldn't even mind being a single mother, as long as I had the time and money to make sure I could do it right. Which, of course, I would, with billions of dollars. But to only have six months to make the decision and put it into action?"

"Actually, you don't even have six months, if that's the deadline," Yeager said oh, so helpfully. "I mean, I'm no expert in baby-making—and thank God for that—but even I know it doesn't always happen the first time. Or the second. Or the third. You're going to need all the time you can get."

Hannah closed her eyes at the reminder of what she already knew. "Thanks a lot, Grandpa. There's nothing like the pressure of a ticking clock to bring a girl's egg delivery to a crawl."

She snapped her eyes open again. Oh, God, did she actually just say that out loud? When she heard Yeager chuckle, she realized she had. Then again, this whole situation was kind of comical. In an over-the-top, stranger-than-fiction, absolutely surreal kind of way.

She leaned forward and banged her head lightly against the table. In some part of her brain, she'd already realized that, if she wanted to inherit this money—and she very much wanted to inherit this money, since it would enable her to realize every dream she'd ever dreamed—she was going to have to make a decision fast and get herself in the family way as soon as possible.

But now that the rest of her brain was getting in on the action, she knew the prospects weren't looking great. She had nothing remotely resembling a boyfriend. She didn't even have a boy who was her friend. And only one attempt at in vitro was way beyond her financial means. She'd already checked that out, too.

Which left visits to a sperm bank, something she'd also been researching online tonight. If necessary, she could afford a few of those—barely—but if none of the efforts took, and she didn't conceive by the six-month deadline, she would have drained what little savings she had. And fifty grand, although an impressive sum, wasn't going to go far in New York City. These things came with no guarantees, especially if her anxiety about everything really did turn her eggs into the same kind of shrinking violets she was.

What Hannah needed was something that could

counter her potentially diminished fertility. A super-tricked-out, ultra-souped-up, hypermasculine testosterone machine that could fairly guarantee to knock her up. And where the hell was she supposed to find a guy like—

She sat back up and looked at Yeager—and the super-tricked-out, ultra-souped-up, hypermasculine body that housed him. Talk about testosterone overload. The guy flew MiG 29s over the Russian tundra for kicks. He'd climbed Mt. Everest. Twice. He served himself up as shark bait *on purpose*, for God's sake. The man probably produced enough testosterone for ten men. If he couldn't put a woman in the family way, nobody could.

Maybe it was the wine. Maybe it was the whiskey. Maybe it was the wine followed by the whiskey. Or maybe it was just the unmitigated terror of having finally discovered who she was and where she belonged and everything she could attain. It wasn't just the reclaiming of a life that had been denied her, but the promise of a happiness she never thought she would have—and realizing she could lose it all in the blink of an eye or the shrink of an egg.

And she heard herself saying, "So, Mr. Novak. Have you ever thought about donating your sperm to a good cause?"

Before he could stop himself, Yeager spat back into his glass a mouthful of whiskey, something that had never happened to him before. Then again, no one had ever asked him about his intentions for his sperm before, either, so he guessed he was entitled to this one social lapse.

As he wiped his chin with his napkin, he tried to tell himself he'd misheard Hannah's question. "Excuse me?" he asked.

"Your sperm," she said, enunciating the word more clearly this time. "Have you ever thought about donating it?"

So much for having misheard her. "Uh…no," he said decisively.

She eyed him intently, her gaze never wavering from his. For a minute he thought she was going to drop it. Then she asked, "Well, would you think about it now?"

"No," he said even more decisively.

Still, she wouldn't let it go. "I mean, if you would consider it—donating it to me, I mean—I'd sign any kind of documents you want me to, to relieve you of all legal and financial obligations for any offspring that might, um, you know, spring off me. And I'd really, really, really, really, really…"

Her voice trailed off and her brows knitted, as if she'd lost track of what she was going to say. Then her expression cleared. A little.

"I'd really appreciate it," she finally finished. "A lot."

He was about to tell her she was delusional. But

another look at her expression, especially her piercing silver-gray eyes—which were a lot less piercing at the moment than they usually were—told him what she really was was drunk. Hell, of course she was drunk. No woman in her right mind would ask a man she barely knew to father her child.

He never should have encouraged her to drink whiskey on top of bad wine. Hannah wasn't the kind of woman who could drink a man under the table, the way women he dated generally were. The only reason she was asking him such a ridiculous question was because her judgment was clouded. He should just let her down gently, explain why what she was asking him to do was a terrible idea, then make sure she got home safely.

He should also, as inconspicuously as possible, scoot both of their drinks out of her reach. Which he did. She didn't even notice, because she was hanging so heavily on his reply.

"Hannah, I… I'm flattered," he finally said. "But it's not a good idea for me to do something like that."

She looked crestfallen. "Why not?"

"Because I'm not good father material."

At this, she looked aghast. "Are you kidding? You're incredible father material. You're smart and interesting and brave and funny and, holy cow, you're *gorgeous*."

He bit back a smile. "Thanks. But those aren't things that necessarily make a good father."

"Maybe not, but they make an *ex*cellent breeder."

He wasn't sure how to respond to that. Part of him was inordinately proud of the suggestion. Another part felt kind of tawdry. Strange—no woman had ever made him feel cheap before.

He pushed the thought away. "Well, I appreciate you considering me that way—" *I think* "—but it's still not a good idea."

"Why not?" she insisted.

There were so many reasons he could give her. There was just no way Yeager was going to be a father at all. Ever. Not in any universe, known or unknown. Not in her dreams or in his. Children were a constant reminder of a person's mortality—nothing marked the passage of time and the steady march to old age better than a child growing by leaps and bounds. The last thing he wanted to be reminded of was that, someday, he would be too old—or too dead—to enjoy life to its fullest. Not to mention that if he knew there was a kid in the world he was responsible for, it might make him more cautious, something that would put a major crimp in his extreme-adventure, thumbing-his-nose-at-death lifestyle. And there was nothing Yeager loved more than his lifestyle.

There was just no way he was going to become a father. Period. No—exclamation point. No—double exclamation point. Triple. Quadruple. Quintuple. Whatever the "uple" was that came after infinity. But, how to make that clear to Hannah?

"It's not a good idea," he said again, more gently this time.

For some reason his softer tone had a greater impact in conveying his opposition than his decisive one. She slumped back in her seat and covered her face with her hands the way she had earlier in her apartment.

He felt that weird tightening in his chest again. But what was he supposed to do? Hannah definitely had a major problem on her hands. But it was *her* problem, not his. She was a resourceful person. She'd figure out what she needed to do. Tomorrow, after the shock had worn off some, she could assess with a clearer head. If she didn't have a boyfriend—and since she'd just asked Yeager to be her sperm donor, it was clear she didn't have a boyfriend—then maybe some other friend with a, um, Y-chromosome would, ah, rise to the occasion. To put it crassly. Or there had to be dozens of sperm banks in New York she could use. Women did that all the time. It was no big deal.

Even if, somehow, Hannah doing that felt like kind of a big deal.

"Come on," he said, "let's get you home."

He withdrew his wallet and threw a handful of bills down on the table. Then, as gently as he could, he pulled her hands away from her face. There were tears in her eyes again, but he did his best to make himself immune to them. He almost succeeded. Then he led her through the bar and out onto the street. It was fully dark now, but there were still plenty of pedestrians. Muted music filtered through the open doors of the bars they passed, and the air was heavy with the aroma of summer in the city.

Hannah said not a word as they made their way back to her apartment. Absently, she withdrew her keys from her purse and promptly dropped them, so Yeager scooped them up and did the honors. It wasn't that hard. She only had three keys on her ring and he lucked into the correct one right off the bat. One of the others opened her front door at the top of the stairs. The third was probably for Cathcart and Quinn.

His own key ring held a dozen keys that he needed to get through a typical week. Hannah only needed three for the whole of her life. But then Hannah lived in one room with one window, too. He pushed her front door open and stood back for her to enter. A family fortune would certainly make her life better. *If* she was able to inherit.

She would be, he assured himself as he followed her into her apartment. She was a smart, capable person. She'd figure out how to make it happen. Eventually.

"Are you going to be okay?" he asked.

She headed to the love seat and folded herself onto

it. "Yeah," she assured him in a way that wasn't at all reassuring.

"You sure?"

She nodded. "Don't forget your shirt."

Damn. Good thing she'd reminded him. He actually had forgotten about it. And it was the whole reason he'd come there tonight. He crossed to the rack to retrieve it.

He'd already paid her the extra hundred he'd promised, but he hadn't paid for the shirt itself. So he asked, "How much do I owe you?"

She cited a price significantly lower than he would have paid had she made the shirt under the auspices of her employer, presumably because of the different fabric. So he pulled out all the bills that remained in his wallet, which was actually more than what the shirt would have cost him at Cathcart and Quinn, and handed them to her.

"That's too much," she said, handing a few bills back.

He started to insist she take them anyway, but something in her voice made him stop. She sounded almost offended that he was giving her more than she asked for. So he returned the bills to his wallet. She stretched out on the love seat, tucked a throw pillow under her head and closed her eyes. He wondered where she slept at night and then noted that the wall behind the love seat looked like it housed a Murphy bed. Lying there the way she was now, she looked even smaller than she usually did, swallowed by the tiny room in which she lived.

Business concluded, it was time for Yeager to go. His flight to the other side of the world left in thirty-six hours. He had a million things to do between now and then. So why was he hesitant to leave Hannah's cramped little apartment that looked at the back of a building across the way?

"I'm not leaving for South Africa until the day after tomorrow," he said. "If you need to talk between now and then, just…"

Just what? he asked himself. If she needed to talk, she should just call him and he'd come right over? Hell, on days as busy as tomorrow was promising to be, he didn't even answer his phone, let alone take on any activities that weren't absolutely essential.

"If you need to talk, you can call me," he told her.

"That's okay," she replied softly, not opening her eyes. "I'll be fine. Thanks."

"You're sure?"

She nodded.

"Okay," he said. And still didn't leave.

She opened her eyes and he felt better when he saw that some of the life had returned to their silvery depths. "Bon voyage," she told him. "Try not to bleed on anything this time, okay?"

He grinned. "I'll see you when I get back."

Because he always saw her when he got back. He invariably had something that needed mending or cleaning. Funny, though, how that was the last thing he was thinking about at the moment. She really did have beautiful eyes.

"Be careful," she told him.

"I told you those are the last words—"

"Break a leg," she amended.

"Actually, that's probably not the best thing to say to an extreme adventurer, either."

"Have fun."

"That's more like it."

Even though he didn't want to, Yeager made himself cross to the front door and open it. Hannah lifted a hand in farewell then he stepped across the threshold and closed the door behind him. Leaving him to focus on all the other things he needed to do before he left town. Instead, as he made his way down Greenpoint Avenue toward the train, Yeager found himself wondering what two eye colors had to mix in a set of parents to make such an interesting combination of gray and silver in their child.

And he wondered if, when Hannah had her baby—and he was sure that somehow, some way, that would definitely happen—her child would have silver-gray eyes, too.

Four

Three weeks after Hannah asked Yeager if he would consider donating his sperm for a worthy cause, she still couldn't believe she'd done it. Every time she remembered that conversation, she was mortified all over again. And she promised herself she would never mix acceptably good Irish whiskey and bad wine products again.

Not that she would be doing that anyway, since she'd taken the plunge and contacted a Manhattan sperm bank to begin the process of artificial insemination. With any luck, she'd be pregnant soon, something that would put an end to imbibing for a while. It would put an end to a lot of things, actually. If—no, when—Hannah became pregnant, she would enter an entirely new phase of her life, one from which she would never be able to backpedal.

She'd spent the entire week following her first conversation with Gus Fiver sorting out her thoughts, weighing the pros and cons and ins and outs of her prospects. And in the end she hadn't been all that surprised to realize that, even more than inheriting a fortune, she wanted to get pregnant because she was ready to start a family—and probably had been for some time.

She'd wanted to be a part of a family her entire life, after all. She'd just always assumed she would need to have a life partner to achieve that. Not only because of the biological requirements, but because of the financial ones, as well. As much as Hannah wanted to have kids, there was no way she could afford to do that on her own with the life she led now. But if she'd had the financial means to raise a child, she would have started a family years ago.

If things worked out the way she now hoped— and they would work out…she hoped—she would not only have the funds to establish Joey & Kit as a driving force in the children's fashion business, she'd also be surrounded by family as she did it. Because if she inherited the funds to raise a child right, then no way was she stopping at one. Hannah wanted a houseful of children. Children who would never, ever, be told they had to leave.

Thank goodness for twenty-first-century medical progress and social mores, enabling women who wanted a family to start one, with or without a life partner.

Which was how Hannah came to be sitting on her love seat three weeks after her first meeting with Gus Fiver, laptop open, chamomile steeping, as she perused all the online forms and documents provided by the sperm bank she would be using. And, wow, there were a lot of them. In addition to the registration form, there was the Agreement to Purchase Donor Sperm form, the Authorization to Release Frozen Sperm form, and the Authorization to Transport Frozen Specimen form. Also, the Sperm Cryopreservation form, the Sperm Storage form, and the Egg/Embryo/Ovarian Tissue Storage form.

And then there was all the stuff she had to read and sign off on. Articles about andrology and semen analysis and sperm-washing techniques. More articles about infectious disease screening and genetic testing and karyotyping. It was all so scientific. So clinical. So…

She sighed. So sterile.

She'd had no idea how much time, work and expense went into baby-making when a person wasn't doing it the old-fashioned way. Still, if this was what it took, she would persevere. What was a little carpal tunnel if it meant there was a family at the end of it? Family was what she'd wanted all her life. Family and security. Now both were within her reach.

Of course she would do whatever she had to do to win both.

Even if it did feel kind of cold, impersonal and dispassionate, which was the last way a child should be conceived.

It didn't matter, she told herself again. All that mattered was that she would be able to start a family and a business and support them both. All that mattered was that she would never be separated from a family—her family—again. All that mattered was that her children would be loved to distraction and grow up in a secure, stable, permanent environment.

Okay. Pep talk over. Hannah had things to do. She had forms to fill out, a donor to choose, an egg to release... Her evening was full. Cracking her knuckles, she went to the Donor Search tab to fill in her specifications. Unfortunately, when she input her preferred traits of Caucasian, blue eyes, black hair, six-feet-plus and postgraduate degree—she knew Yeager had a master's in Geopolitics, not that she was trying to recreate Yeager or anything like that—the search resulted in *No donors available at this time*.

She tried again, leaving out the part about six-feet-plus. Still nothing. Okay, fine. The donor didn't *have* to have a master's degree. Again, no results. Ultimately the closest she could get to her original preferences was a five-foot-eleven, green-eyed brunet with a BA in philosophy.

She had nearly finished filling out the initial application form when her intercom buzzer rang. Since she wasn't expecting anyone for a pickup from Joey & Kit, she figured it was someone looking for her across-the-hall neighbor Jeannette, who seemed to know everyone in New York, though no one in New York could seem to remember that Jeannette was in unit A, not B.

Hannah went to press the buzzer, ready to tell whoever it was that they had the wrong apartment. Before she had the chance, she heard a familiar voice coming over the intercom. "Hannah? It's Yeager. Are you home?"

After a moment of stunned surprise she replied, "Yeah, come on up," and buzzed him in.

She knew a moment's chagrin when she remembered she was already in her pajamas. Or, at least, what passed for pajamas on her—cotton pants decorated with fat cartoon sheep and a purple T-shirt whose sleeves she'd cut off to use for trim on one of her Joey & Kit creations. But she didn't have time to change, so she opened her front door and stepped into the hallway at the top of the stairs to wait for Yeager.

He climbed them sluggishly, his left hand dragging along the rail beside him. She immediately knew something was wrong. That was hammered home when he finally reached the landing and looked at her. His blue eyes, usually so animated and laughing, were flat and empty. His hair was unkempt. He was unshaved. He looked as if he'd slept in his khaki trousers and white shirt, which he hadn't even tucked in.

"Hey," she said gently by way of a greeting when he topped the last step.

"Hi," he said softly.

She was about to ask him what he was doing there, but something about his demeanor prevented her. Whatever his reason for coming to her place tonight, he would get to it eventually. Right now, he didn't seem inclined to talk.

"Come on in."

She entered first, waiting for him to pass her before closing the door behind him. He strode slowly to the love seat and heavily sat, staring straight ahead but not seeming to see anything.

Hannah sat beside him, closing her laptop and moving it to the floor to make room. "I'm sorry. I'm all out of bad wine," she said, hoping to lighten his mood. "Would you like something else? Coffee? Tea?"

He shook his head, not even smiling at her attempt at levity. "No, that's okay. Thanks."

Finally he turned to look at her. She waited for him to start talking, but he remained silent. So she asked the same question he'd asked three weeks ago, the one that had led to her spilling her troubles out to him.

"Is everything okay?"

He was silent for another moment. Then he said, "Not really." His dark brows arrowed downward and he met her gaze levelly. "I need to ask you a question."

Heat pooled in her belly at the seriousness of his tone. Even so, she told him, "Sure."

There was another bout of silence as he studied her face with great interest. And then, out of nowhere, he asked, "Is that offer to father your child still on the table?"

Yeager really hadn't meant to just blurt out the question the way he had. He'd intended to preface it with all the other things he had to tell Hannah first, so it wouldn't come as such a shock to her when he finally asked it. Then again, after what had happened in Nunavut—and how he'd felt since—the realization that he wanted to ask the question still came as a shock to him. Even more of a shock was how much he hoped she wouldn't tell him he was too late.

It had just been a hell of a few weeks, that was all. The trip to South Africa had been everything he'd hoped for and then some, one rush of adrenaline after another, an intoxicating brew of exuberance and euphoria. But the trip to Nunavut, the one that was supposed to have been no business and all pleasure…

"Yeah, the offer is still good," Hannah said, interrupting his thoughts, something for which he was grateful. "I mean, if you're the one who's interested, it is."

"I am," he replied immediately.

Although he could see surprise reflected in her silvery eyes, her voice was level and matter-of-fact when she replied.

"O-o-okay."

Well, except for the nervous stammer.

She wanted to know why he'd changed his mind—the look in her eyes made that clear, too. He waited for her to ask, but the question that came out instead was, "Are you, um, sober at the moment?"

For the first time in weeks he smiled. Not a big smile, but it was good to know he could still manage one. "Stone cold," he assured her.

"Okay," she said again, more steadily this time. "Just wanted to make sure."

"You want to know what's brought about this one-eighty, don't you?"

She nodded. He sighed. In spite of having gone over it in his head a million times, he still didn't know how to explain it. Ultimately he decided to begin with what had reawakened the idea of fathering a child with Hannah in his head.

"I lost a good friend a couple of weeks ago," he said.

"And by 'lost,' you mean…"

"He died."

"Oh, Mr. Novak. I am so sorry."

"Yeager," he corrected her, since this wasn't going to be the kind of conversation a person had with someone who only knew him on a last-name basis. "Call me Yeager, Hannah. What's your last name?" he added, since this wasn't the kind of conversation a person had with someone he only knew on a first-name basis, either.

Surprise flashed in her eyes again but she recovered quickly and told him. "Robinson."

Hannah Robinson. The name suited her. Sturdy, no-nonsense.

She tried again. "I'm so sorry for your loss... Yeager."

"Thanks," he replied, marveling at the curl of pleasure that wound through him when she spoke his name. Where had that come from?

He waited for her to ask what had happened, but she didn't. Hannah Robinson was evidently the sort of person who didn't pry. Normally it would have been something else he loved about her. But it would help to have her guide him through what he had to say.

"You remember how I told you I was going to Nunavut to climb Mount Thor with friends?" he began.

She nodded.

"While we were there, one of those friends... One of them had a... There was an accident," he finally said. "We're still not sure how it happened. I mean,

I guess it doesn't matter how it happened. But he... he fell to his death."

"Oh, no..."

"One minute he was there and the next..."

"Oh, Yeager."

Something in his chest grew tight and cold, a sensation that was becoming too familiar. So he did what he always did when that feeling threatened to overwhelm him. He pushed it away.

And he made himself continue. "He and I met in college. We started Ends of the Earth together. I had the head for business and he was the tech whiz. After we incorporated, I became President and CEO, and he was VP and Chief Technology Officer." He grinned. "He was the only VP Chief Officer of anything for the first three years. He was a great guy. A good friend. Full of life. I still can't believe he's—"

Yeager felt himself starting to blather, so he shut himself up. Hannah seemed to understand, because she scooted closer to him on the love seat. She extended a hand toward him, hesitated, then settled it gently on his forearm. It was a careful, innocent touch, but he felt it to the depths of his soul. Maybe because it was the first comforting gesture someone had made to him since he'd returned to the States.

Hell, even before then. No one ever tried to comfort Yeager. For one thing, he had the kind of life that didn't invite comforting, since it included everything a human being could ever want. For another thing, he had barriers in place that kept people far enough away from him to prevent them from doing things like offer comfort. At least, he'd always thought he had barriers like that in place. Hannah, however, evidently couldn't see them.

"Did he have a family?" she asked.

Yeager shook his head. But her question was the perfect segue for where he needed to steer the conversation. Maybe she'd be able to guide him through this, after all.

"His dad died when he was still a baby and he lost his mom a couple of years ago. He didn't have any brothers or sisters. It was another thing that bonded us when we first met, since I was an only child, too."

"Sounds like you two were a couple of lone wolves who made your own pack," Hannah said.

She lightly squeezed his arm and smiled a gentle smile. That was nice of her. Not many people tried that with Yeager, either.

"Yeah," he said. "Back in the day, being lone wolves suited us. Hell, last month, being lone wolves suited us. He was no more the marrying kind than I am. But suddenly…" Yeager hesitated again. "Suddenly, being a lone wolf has its drawbacks. I mean, there's nothing left of him in the world now, you know? Nothing left behind after his death that might bring comfort to the people who knew him and cared about him in life."

"But you must have some wonderful memories," Hannah said.

"I do. But that's just it. All any of us who knew him has is memories. Memories that will gradually fade then die when we do. After that, there won't be anything left of him at all. No indication that he ever even existed. He was such a larger-than-life person. He lived with such passion and exhilaration. For there to be nothing left now that was a part of him… That just seems wrong, you know?"

Hannah loosened her hold on Yeager's arm but didn't let go. There was something in her eyes now that told him she wasn't following him. Then again, she wasn't the kind of person who wanted to make her mark on the world. She'd said as much herself that time she'd told him what a prudent life she led.

But Yeager did want to make his mark on the world. He wanted to be remembered—and remembered well—long after he was gone. He wanted to leave behind a legacy of some kind. He'd never been sure exactly what kind of legacy, but it had to be something that people could point to and say, "Yeager Novak was here." Something that would keep his name and his spirit alive for years. For generations. Hell, forever. He'd always assumed he had plenty of time to figure out the particulars. But now he understood, too well, that life was fleeting, and he'd damned well better make the best of it because it could be snatched away anytime, without any kind of warning.

"I guess I just always thought he was immortal." Yeager tried again to explain. "That he'd go on forever. I thought both of us would. But now I know the clock is ticking on the immortality thing, and I realize that, if I died tomorrow, the same thing would happen to me that's happened to him. There'd be nothing of me in the world anymore."

"You want to leave behind a legacy after you're gone," she said.

He nodded, stunned that she'd used the same word he'd been thinking. "Yeah."

"And you think a child would be a good legacy."

"Yes."

She hesitated a moment, her gaze never leaving his. "There are other kinds of legacies that would—"

"No, there aren't," he interrupted, fearful she might be reconsidering her offer. "Other legacies can deteriorate or fall apart or be stored somewhere and forgotten about. But a child to carry on after I'm gone will be a literal part of me. And then his— or her—children will be a literal part of me. And their children will be, too. And then their children, and their children, and their children…" He forced a smile then was surprised to realize it wasn't forced at all. "When you get right down to it, Hannah, having a kid to carry on after you're gone damned near makes you immortal."

She smiled back. And something in that smile made Yeager feel better than he'd felt in a very long time. "I guess you're right."

"So I started thinking about that," he continued. "And I started warming to the idea of fathering a child." He might as well admit the rest, since that part had been as surprising as anything else. "I started warming to the idea of fathering *your* child."

Because he'd thought about all the other women he knew who might be amenable to that—there were actually more than a few—and realized Hannah was the only one he could honestly imagine doing the job right.

"If," he concluded, "like I said, the offer is still open."

"It's still open," she assured him again, even more quickly than she had the first time.

"Then I'd like to humbly offer my chromosomes to your cause," he told her.

He hesitated again, not sure how she was going to feel about the next part since it included conditions. He was sure she'd already had enough of those placed on her by her grandfather.

So, being careful for the first time he could remember, he said tentatively, "I have three conditions for my offer, though."

She released his arm. She didn't drop it like a hot potato or anything, but she did withdraw her hand. She also scooted a little bit away from him on the love seat and straightened her spine—a couple more telling gestures.

"What conditions?" she asked a little warily.

He didn't blame her for her caution. But he wasn't going to go into this thing lightly any more than she was.

"Number one," he began, "I'd like you to name the child after the friend I lost."

Her posture eased some. "Okay."

"Don't you want to make sure he didn't have a weird name, or one that's gender-specific?"

She smiled again; a softer smile that changed her whole demeanor. For the first time Yeager was seeing that she wasn't all diligence and pragmatism. There was a lot of gentleness and warmth there, too.

"It doesn't matter," she said. "It's a sweet, loving gesture you want to make, Yeager, and I would never say no to a sweet, loving gesture. There are too few of them in the world."

"His name was Thomas Brennan," Yeager said. "Tommy Brennan. I figure Brennan would suit a boy or girl."

She let it settle in then nodded. "Brennan Novak. That's a good name."

"You don't have to give your baby my last name," Yeager said. Even though, for some reason, he suddenly kind of liked the idea.

"Yeah. I kinda think I do," she said with a smile

that was cryptic this time. "He or she will be Brennan Robinson Novak. That's a very good name."

"That is a very good name, now that you mention it," he agreed, feeling strangely gentle and warm himself.

"Okay, so that's settled," she said. "What else?"

His second condition wasn't going to be quite as easy to put on the table as the first. Even so, there was no reason to gloss over it. He might be seeing a softer side of Hannah this evening, but she was still the most practical woman he knew—something he suddenly kind of loved about her—and he knew she would appreciate his forthrightness.

"The second condition is that you and I have to make your baby the old-fashioned way, not with vials and test tubes and syringes. Having an adventurer's legacy come about by syringe just isn't very... I don't know. Adventurous."

"I guess I can see that."

"I'd just prefer to ensure my legacy—and honor Tommy's name—by having this baby come about through natural means and during an epic adventure. That just feels right for some reason. So you and I are going to have to have sex, Hannah. And we're going to have do it in epic proportions on some kind of epic adventure. I hope your passport is up to date."

He was relieved when she didn't look like she wanted to negotiate on the matter. In fact, from her expression, it kind of looked as though she wanted to get started right away.

She blinked a few times then said, pretty amenably, "Okay. If we *have* to."

"We do."

She was silent for another moment. "What's the third condition?"

The third condition was the only one he feared Hannah wouldn't agree to, and it was the most important one. At least, to Yeager. But where her refusal of the first condition would have been disappointing, but not a deal-breaker, and her refusal of the second was never really in doubt—all modesty aside, since he didn't have any, and he'd seen the way she looked at him in the shop when he was half-dressed—his third condition was sacrosanct. If she didn't go along with this one, then he would pull out of the deal.

"I want to be…" he began then changed his mind. "No, I *have* to be a part of the child's life." He hurried to clarify before she could object. "I won't be an intrusion in your life, Hannah. Hell, I don't want to alter my life very much, either. I'll definitely keep adventuring. You'll call the shots when it comes to child rearing. But I want my son or daughter to know me, and I want to know my son or daughter. Yes, you will be the child's primary parent. But I want regular visitation, and when the child is old enough, I want to include him or her in my travels whenever and wherever possible."

He thought she would tell him she'd need time to think about that. Ask if she could she sleep on it and get back to him tomorrow. Instead she told him without hesitation, "No problem."

His surprise that she conceded so easily must have been obvious, because she quickly explained.

"Yeager, I'm the last person to deny a child the right to know his or her parents, since I never knew my own and would have loved nothing more than to have had them in my life. I mean, yeah, it sounds like my father left a lot to be desired as a human being, but I would have still liked the opportunity to know him. Or at least know who he was when I was growing up. Good or bad, a lot of our identity is linked to our parents and where they come from. I never had a chance to know that part of my identity. And I never will. Of course I won't deny you the chance to be a part of your child's life. And I won't deny your child a chance to be a part of your life."

Yeager didn't know what to say. So he only said, "Thanks."

For a long time they sat on the love seat, staring at each other, as if neither knew what to do next. Then again, speaking for himself, Yeager had no idea what to do next. Naturally, he knew the mechanics that went into making a baby. But he also knew there were other things to consider beyond the act itself. Things like timing and opportunity, for instance. He had a pretty hectic schedule mapped out for the next six months. Not that he thought they'd need the full six months to conceive, since they were both young and healthy, but he did need to make some arrangements for the foreseeable future where the workings of Hannah's biological clock were concerned. He'd be there for her whenever she needed him, but, as was the case with living life, he needed some kind of timetable to work with for generating life, too.

"So," he finally said, "what do we do next?"

She lifted her shoulders a little self-consciously then let them drop. When she did, her shirt shifted enough to drop over one shoulder, exposing the delectable skin of her collarbone and the faint upper curve of one breast. In addition to having beautiful eyes, Hannah had some beautiful skin. Even if some of it was, at the moment, clothed in cartoon sheep.

"Well, you said we have to have sex," she replied softly, "so I guess we have sex."

Yeager was still pondering the creaminess of her breast when her words finally registered and, bizarrely, he knew a moment's panic. "Wait, what? You mean right now?"

Why was he panicking? He should have been— and normally would have been—standing up to go to work on his fly by now. But he could tell he wasn't the only one responding uncharacteristically. Hannah was blushing furiously. And seeing that made something inside him that hadn't been warm in a very long time go absolutely incandescent. He'd never seen a woman blush before. Certainly not with the adeptness with which Hannah managed it. And where before a woman blushing would have been off-putting, with her, it was…not. On the contrary…

"No, not right now," she said. "I'm not… I won't be…" She expelled a restless sigh. "My body has a schedule for this kind of thing," she finally said.

"Yeah, I know that much," he assured her. "But I need to know if I should book an extra ticket for my trip to Argentina next week or if we'll be…you know…before then."

You know? he echoed incredulously to himself. Had he just referred to sex as *you know*? What, was he twelve years old? Hell, he hadn't even referred to sex as *you know* when he was twelve.

Hannah blushed again. And that hot place inside him grew hotter still. What was going on with his body tonight? She was the one who was supposed to be experiencing physiological changes, not him.

"It won't be before next week," she told him. "I've mapped out my cycle for the next three months as best I can, and although there's going to be some give-and-take there, because I'm not exactly regular, I can say that the middle of next week will be prime time. But I can't go to Argentina with you," she added. "I don't have a passport."

She didn't have a passport? Yeager marveled. What kind of person didn't have a passport? Oh, right. A seamstress in Sunnyside, New York, who had to work two jobs to make ends meet.

"Okay, we can get around that," he said. "I can send one of my senior agents on the Argentina trip in my place and stay here in the States. But you need to get a passport ASAP in case this first time doesn't work. Like I said, I really think, to honor Tommy's spirit and make this a legacy in the truest sense, the child should be conceived on an epic adventure."

"And I think that's a gallant and honorable gesture," Hannah told him. "But you need to find something epic to do here in New York. Because I can't take time off from Cathcart and Quinn."

"We have to go someplace other than New York. There's no epic adventure to be had here."

She gaped at him. "Are you out of your mind? New York is nothing but epic adventures. Have you taken the subway lately? Walked through the Garment District after dark? Eaten one of those chimi-churro-changa-chiladas from Taco Taberna? Nobody gets out alive after ingesting one of those things."

"Look, I'll figure out something. But you're going to have to take some time off from work next week, because we're going on an adventure, and that means getting out of New York. Do you have a specific day for us to…?" He would *not* say *you know* again. "A specific day for us to, um…"

"Wednesday," she hurriedly replied.

"Great," he said. "That gives me a few days to figure out where we'll be going."

"But I can't afford to take any days off from work," she insisted. "I barely save anything from my paycheck as it is. Speaking of, I don't have enough money to travel anywhere, anyway. I'm not a billionaire's granddaughter yet. Not financially, at least. I need that paycheck, and I can't lose my job in case you and I aren't successful at—"

"Oh, we'll be successful," he stated in no uncertain terms.

"You'll excuse me if I'm not as full of bravado as you are," she said.

"It's not bravado I'm full of," he assured her.

She sighed. "Fine. You're a raging tower of testosterone."

"Damn straight."

For the first time that evening she looked a little defeated. "Maybe I'm not quite as confident about my own contribution to the venture as you are of yours."

He wanted to tell her she had nothing to worry about there. Hannah Robinson was more woman than most women he knew. Funny that he was only now noticing that. "If it will help, I could talk to your bosses for you. Tell them I need you to do some work for me out of town for a couple of days or something and that I'll make it worth their while."

She was shaking her head before he even finished.

"I appreciate it, but I'll talk to Mr. Cathcart and Mr. Quinn myself. Maybe they'll let me work over next weekend to make up for being out a couple of days during the week."

"But you shouldn't have to—"

"It's okay, Yeager. I've made my own way in the world this long. I can take care of myself."

He remembered how she'd told him she'd grown up in New York's foster care system. She hadn't gone into detail about it. But anyone who'd gone through something like that and come out on the other side as happy and well-adjusted as Hannah seemed to be could definitely take care of herself. There was a part of Yeager, though, that really wanted to help her out. He was surprised at the depth of his disappointment that she wouldn't let him.

He pushed those thoughts away. For now. Something told him he'd be coming back to them in the not too distant future. "So I should make plans for us to be away for...how long?" he asked.

Her gaze deflected from his, moving to something over his right shoulder, and she bit her lip in the thoughtful way that had intrigued him so much at the shop that day. It had the same heated effect on him now, except stronger, making a part of him twitch that had never twitched in Hannah's presence before. Interesting.

"Well, according to my reading," she said, "There's a three-day window for me to be at peak,

and it's best for you to wait twenty-four hours between attempts to, um, replenish your, uh, stock."

Yeah, right. Like that was going to be necessary
for him. "Okay, so we'll need three nights." For some
reason he suddenly kind of liked the idea of spending
that much time with Hannah. "We can leave early
Tuesday morning and come back Friday. Let me see
what I can arrange."

"But—"

"Kauai is the obvious choice for domestic adventure," he decided immediately. "The twelve-hour
flight to Hawaii makes that kind of difficult, under
the circumstances, though."

"But, Yeager—"

"Maybe the Grand Canyon or Yosemite. Or there
are a few places in Maine that would be closer. Hell,
even the parts of the Adirondacks might work."

"But, Yeager, I—"

"Don't worry about it, Hannah. I'll take care of all
the arrangements. It's what I do for a living."

"It's not the arrangements I'm worried about," she
told him. "It's the expenses."

"Don't worry about that part, either. I'll cover
those, too. I'll take care of everything."

At this, she looked angry. "The hell you will. This
is my baby, too."

Why was she getting so mad? It was ridiculous
to argue about this. Yeager had more money than
he knew what to do with. He could afford this bet-

ter than Hannah could, and he was the one who was insisting that the conception be an adventure in its own right.

Even so, he relented. "Fine. You can pay me back after you inherit."

"But what if I don't—"

"You will," he assured her. Because there was no question about that.

She thought about it for a moment and then finally nodded. "Keep an itemized list of what you spend for this," she said. "Every mile, every meal, every minute. And bill me for my half of everything after I conceive. I intend to pay my fair share."

Of course she did. Because even with the flashing eyes, the erotic lip nibble and the luscious skin, she was still, at heart, practical, pragmatic Hannah.

"Agreed," he said. And then, before she could offer any more objections, he told her, "I'll pick you up here Tuesday morning and return you here Friday afternoon. Pack for being outdoors, for warm and cool weather both. Bring clothes and shoes for walking and climbing. And sunscreen. I'll take care of everything else."

Well, except for the second set of chromosomes that would be necessary for conceiving a child. He'd need Hannah for that. Weird. Yeager hadn't needed anyone for a long time. Since his parents' deaths, he'd come to rely only on himself and had figured it would be that way for the rest of his life. He'd gotten to a point where he almost resented relying on other people for something. But needing Hannah… and needing her for this… He wasn't resentful at all. Needing her felt oddly appropriate. Even natural.

Probably, it was some primal instinct making him react that way. Man's inherent need to carry on the species that dated back to the beginning of time. Yeah, that had to be it. Because, seriously, what else could it be?

Five

When Yeager had told Hannah to pack for walking and hiking, she figured that meant they would
be walking and hiking. So what was she doing sitting in a four-seater inflatable raft, wrapped in a
life jacket and staring down a river in North Carolina that would eventually become miles and miles
of whitewater?

She looked at Yeager, who was still on the dock,
double-checking whatever he needed to double-check
before they hurtled headlong into self-destruction.
Not that he seemed concerned about that. Then
again, had it not been for the raging aquatic disas-
ter ahead, she might have been just as Zen-like as he
was, because North Carolina was the greenest, the

bluest, the most gorgeous and peaceful place she'd ever seen.

The closest Hannah ever came to the Great Out-doors was Central Park, a place she didn't even have an opportunity to visit as often as she liked. And as beautiful as it was, it was often crowded with people and was still surrounded by towering skyscrapers and bumper-to-bumper buses and cabs, its sky criss-crossed with air traffic. This was her first taste of actual, honest-to-god nature. And it was incredible.

Evergreens sprouted along both sides of the river, a hundred feet high, stretching into a cloudless blue sky that was as clear and bright as a gemstone. And the air. Holy cow, it was amazing. Warm and lan-guid, touched with just a hint of humidity and filled with the scent of pine and earth and something vaguely, but not unpleasantly, fishy. Although the water wasn't yet rough enough to be called white-water, it whirled and gurgled past in a hurry, tug-ging at the raft and vying with the wind for whose rush of sound was most eloquent.

It was hard to believe fewer than six hours had passed since Yeager had picked her up in Queens in a shiny black car, complete with driver. They'd driven to a small airport in New Jersey where they'd boarded a private jet—because, of course, Ends of the Earth had its own private jet—then made the two-hour flight to Asheville, North Carolina. It was

Hannah's first time on a plane and her first time out-side New York.

They'd ventured into Asheville long enough to eat breakfast, and although the town was small by New York standards, it was still kind of urban and cosmo-politan, so it hadn't felt *too* different from Queens. Well, except for the great green bumps of mountain surrounding it. But as they'd driven away from the city in the Land Rover that had been waiting for them on arrival, everything—*everything*—had changed.

So much green. So much sky. So little traffic. So few people. The farther they'd traveled, the more iso-lated they'd become, even on the highway. And once they'd exited the interstate, they might as well have been the only two people on the planet. Instinctively, Hannah had rolled down her window and turned her face to the breeze, closing her eyes to feel the warmth of the sun on her face and inhaling great gulps of air that was unlike anything she'd ever drawn into her body.

Yeager had driven up, up, up into the mountains, until they arrived at a secluded dock on the Chat-tanooga River, where they'd found the very raft in which she now sat. It had been conjured, presum-ably, by magic, along with its contents of life jackets, cooler and oars, because there wasn't another soul in sight. Just Hannah and Yeager and the primordial earth spirits she was sure still lived here.

She eyed the river again, battling a gnarl of fear

curling up in her belly. He'd told her he would go easy on her this trip and make the outing low-risk, since she was still new to the adventure thing. He'd promised the danger to her would be nonexistent. She wasn't sure she believed him. There was a bend in the river not far ahead, and she was worried about what lay around it. Where her idea of staying safe was not climbing into a tiny inflatable raft on a raging river—or, you know, *any* river—Yeager's idea of safety probably meant there was enough oxygen to last ten minutes or fewer scorpions than usual.

Potato, potahto.

"Are you sure this is safe?" she asked him.

He was shrugging his dun-colored life jacket over a skintight black T-shirt and khaki cargo shorts. Well-worn hiking boots, a gimme cap emblazoned with the Ends of the Earth logo and aviator sunglasses completed the ensemble. He looked every inch the wealthy epic adventurer. She could almost smell the testosterone oozing from every pore. She gazed down at her attire—cut-offs and a T-shirt she'd received for making a donation to public radio. Coupled with her sneakers and retro cat-eye sunglasses, and with her unruly hair stuffed into an even more unruly ponytail, she was going to go out on a limb and say she did *not* look like a wealthy epic adventurer. Especially in a life jacket that was two sizes too big for her.

"Of course it's safe," he assured her. "The rap-

ids here are only Class Two. They have camps for
middle-schoolers along this stretch."

Hannah eyed the river again. Yeah, right, she
thought. Feral middle schoolers, maybe. Who'd been
raised by wolves. She couldn't imagine any halfway responsible parent allowing their child anywhere
near a river like this. Maybe she'd been too hasty in
agreeing to Yeager's condition that they leave New
York. She'd rather their adventure involve eating
sushi from a food truck or crossing Queens Bou-
levard against the light. Now *that* was living dangerously.

She tried to object again. "But—"

"It's fine, Hannah," Yeager interrupted before she
had the chance, cinching the belt of his life jacket.
Then he threw her one of those smiles that always
kindled something inside her. "You'll have fun. I
promise. C'mon. Do you really think I'd endanger
the mother of my child?"

The warmth inside her sparked hotter at that. The
mother of Yeager Novak's child. That was what she
would be for the rest of her life if everything went
the way it was supposed to. What a weird concept.
What they were planning would bond the two of
them together forever. She'd realized that when she'd
accepted his last condition, of course, but she was
only now beginning to understand exactly what
that meant. The man standing above her looking
like some omnipotent earth god would be moving

in and out of her life *forever*. Was she really, truly, sure she wanted that?

He hopped down into the raft with her, making it rock back and forth enough for her to seize the ropes on its sides nearest her. Her stomach pitched. If she had ever doubted that she wasn't the risk-taking type—and, actually, she had never doubted that at all—she was now certain. They hadn't even left the dock yet and she was already bracing for a spectacular death.

Yeager leaned across the raft, reaching past her to grab a strap she hadn't even noticed was there. He tugged it across her lap and latched it to another one on her other side, effectively securing her in place. She should have been grateful there were seat belts in the raft. Instead, all she could do was panic that now she would drown if the damned thing tipped over.

"What do I do if—"

"The raft won't invert," he interrupted, reading her mind. Again. "The way it's designed, that's impossible. Not to mention—in case I haven't already— this part of the river is in no way dangerous."

Ever the optimist—kind of—Hannah countered, "Nothing is impossible."

Yeager grinned again. "You getting hurt on this trip is."

"Then why do I have to wear a seat belt?" she asked. "If this is as safe as you say it is, then how come even you put on a life jacket?"

"I'm an adventurer, Hannah. I'm not stupid."

Before she could say anything more, he threw off the last line and the raft was moving away from the dock. Hannah opened her mouth to scream—it might be her last chance to draw breath, after all— then realized they were only going about five miles an hour. If that. The raft floated along the water serenely, hitting the occasional gentle bump before turning a bit and gliding forward again.

Yeager held one oar deftly in both hands, maneuvering it first on one side of the raft then the other, steering it simultaneously forward and toward the center of the river. As they gradually picked up speed, so did the wind, until it was buffeting her hair around her face in a way that was actually kind of pleasant. She shoved it aside and gripped the ropes on the sides of the raft, but more out of reflex than because she was actually frightened. They really weren't going very fast and their surroundings really were beautiful.

For long moments they simply glided along the river, the raft rising and falling gently with the swells, turning left, then right, as Yeager guided it forward. Eventually, though, the water did grow rough and the raft's movements became more irregular and jarring. But he handled it expertly, switching the oar from right to left to keep the raft on track. Water splashed up over the sides, wetting Hannah's feet and face, but instead of being alarmed, she thrilled at the sensation. Every new jolt of the raft or pull of the current sent a wave of adrenaline shooting through her, making her pulse dance and her heart race. By the time the water began to cascade over the side of the raft, soaking her legs and arms, her entire body was buzzing with sensations unlike any she had ever experienced before. She held on tighter, but instead of panic it was elation that bubbled up inside her.

And then the water grew very rough and the raft was pitching over rocks and shoals, spinning and leaping and crashing down again. Water splashed fully over both sides of the craft, dowsing both of them. But instead of fearful, Hannah felt joyful. Especially when she saw how Yeager reacted to what must have been a minor feat of derring-do for him. He was grinning in a way she'd never seen him grin before, with a mix of ecstasy and exhilaration and exuberance, as if being right here, in this moment, was the absolute pinnacle of experience—and she was a part of it. Such pure, unadulterated happiness was contagious, and she was swept up into it as fiercely as he was, until she was whooping with laughter.

The journey continued for miles; the river, by turns, as turbulent as a whirlpool and as smooth as glass. During the smooth times, Hannah marveled at the scenery and the wildlife—She saw her first deer! Three of them! Right there on the riverbank!—and asked Yeager what kind of bird that was flying above them and how big pine trees could grow, and did it snow here in the winter. During the turbulent times, he schooled her in how to use her oar and laughed with her whenever she turned the raft backward—which was often.

By the time they reached the end of the course two hours after starting it, Hannah felt more alive than she'd ever felt in her life. As Yeager steered them toward a dock much like the one from which they'd departed, she was keenly disappointed that the ride was coming to an end. So when he slung a rope over a wooden post to secure the raft and turned to look at her to gauge her reaction, she responded in the only way she knew how.

"Can we do it again?" she asked eagerly.

Yeager could hardly believe that the Hannah at the end of their ride was the same one who'd climbed so carefully into the raft upriver. He'd never seen her smile like she was now, with such spirit and wonderment and…something else, something he wasn't sure he could identify, something there probably wasn't even a word for because it was so uniquely Hannah. She just looked more animated than he'd ever seen her, more carefree, more full of life.

Happy. She just looked happy. And he thought it odd that, as many times as he'd seen her and had conversations with her, and she'd seemed contented enough, she'd never really looked happy until now.

Then her question finally registered and he shook the other thoughts out of his brain. Or, at least, tried to. There was something about Hannah's newly found happiness that wouldn't quite leave him.

"We can't go again," he told her. "At least, not from here. We have to hike back upriver first."

She looked a little dejected at that.

"But we can go again tomorrow, if you want to."

"I want to," she immediately replied. Her smile brightened again and something inside Yeager grew brighter, too.

He stood, extending a hand to her. "Come on," he said. "We can do a little exploring before lunch."

She unhooked her safety belt and settled her hand in his, and he pulled her to standing, too. When he did, the raft rolled toward the dock a bit, pitching Hannah forward, into him. Instinctively he settled his hands on her hips as hers splayed open over his chest. Her touch was gentle, but he felt it to the depths of his soul. His hands tightened on her hips and, not sure why he did it, he dipped his head to kiss her. She gasped when he did, and he took advantage of her reaction to deepen the kiss, tasting her leisurely, taking his time to enjoy it. And he did enjoy it. A lot.

Hannah seemed to enjoy it, too, because, without missing a beat, she kissed him back, curling her fingers into the fabric of his shirt to pull him closer. He felt her heart beating hard against his torso, heard the catch of her breath, inhaled the earthy scent of her, becoming more intoxicated by her with each passing second.

He would have taken her right there, right then, shedding their clothes in the raft and settling her naked in his lap astride him. He was already envisioning just how erotic the union would be, but she ended the kiss—with clear reluctance—and pushed herself away from him as far as she could in the small raft. Her face was flushed and her breathing came in rough, irregular gasps. What was weird was that Yeager's breathing was ragged and uneven, too. It was just a kiss, he reminded himself. No big deal. He'd kissed dozens of women. Kisses were nothing but a prelude. There was no reason for him to feel so breathless. So weightless. So senseless.

"We, um, we should probably wait until tonight," she said softly. "Just to keep things as close to Wednesday as possible."

Right. They were on a schedule here. Yeager understood schedules. His entire life was scheduled. Of course they should wait until tonight to ensure optimum results. Even if he suddenly didn't want to wait. His *body* didn't want to wait, he hastily corrected himself. What had just happened between him and Hannah was just a chemical reaction to a physical stimulus. He himself could wait just fine. It was only sex. No problem waiting until tonight.

Even if tonight seemed way too far away.

"You, uh, said something about exploring?" she asked tentatively, her breathing still a little frayed.

Yeager nodded. "Right. Then we can hike farther downstream to where we'll be camping."

"Which is how far?"

"About three miles."

Her mouth dropped open at that. "We're going to hike three miles?"

"Piece a cake," he told her. "It'll be a walk in the park."

She shook her head. "I've walked in the park lots of times. *That's* a walk in the park. Three miles over rugged terrain is—"

"A great way to build up an appetite," he finished for her. He'd let her decide for herself what kind of appetite he was talking about.

Evidently she knew exactly what kind he meant, because color suffused her face again. He'd never seen a woman with such a propensity for blushing. It should have been a turnoff. Yeager liked women who were as audacious and intrepid as he was. But something about Hannah's seeming innocence tugged at a part of him where he wasn't used to feeling things.

Before she could object again, he cinched her waist tighter and lifted her easily up onto the dock, setting her down on her ass as she sputtered in surprise. Then he unfastened the cooler from its mooring in the raft and raised it to the dock, too, placing it beside her. After hoisting himself up effortlessly, he stood and extended a hand to her as he had before. This time, though, he was more careful when he pulled her up alongside him.

Careful, he echoed to himself. He was actually being careful with Hannah. He was never careful with anyone. Anything. Careful was the last thing he ever wanted to be. But then, Hannah was a careful person, and what the two of them were trying to do—create a life together—took care. That was all there was to his reaction. It wasn't like he'd actually begun to, well, *care* for her. No more than he had before, anyway.

The dock was attached to a clearing on the riverbank that disappeared into the forest a few hundred feet away. Yeager was familiar with the area and knew it was rife with common fossils and less common arrowheads, so they shed their shoes to dry in a patch of sunshine and spent some time looking around. When he pointed out a handful of brachiopods and trilobites to Hanna, he might as well have been pouring diamonds into her lap, so delighted was her reaction. He reminded himself again that, in spite of her rocky upbringing, she'd led a fairly sheltered life. It was hard to fathom the contradiction. Hannah just seemed like such an anomaly sometimes.

By the time they finished lunch, their clothes and shoes were dry. Yeager packed the remnants of their meal in the cooler and secured it back in the moored raft, then rejoined Hannah on the dock.

"Don't we need to take those with us?" she asked.

He shook his head. "Someone will be coming for them later."

"The same someone who dropped them off at the first dock?"

Now he nodded. "Ends of the Earth contracts with other travel professionals all over the world. I found one in Raleigh that got everything set up for us here, from where we started in the raft to where we'll be camping. They'll pick up the Land Rover, too, and deliver it to the campsite so we'll have it if we need it."

She eyed him thoughtfully. "You know, when you said we'd be having an epic adventure, I had a picture of us machete-ing our way through the Everglades while dodging alligators or hang gliding across the Grand Canyon. I wasn't planning on coolers full of lobster and San Pellegrino and Land Rovers at our disposal."

Yeager smiled. "Yeah, well, normally machete-ing among alligators *is* the kind of trip Ends of the Earth puts together. The hang gliding is more likely to happen over an active volcano."

She started to laugh, then realized he was serious.

"Anyway, I'm having to break you in gently," he pointed out. Not to mention he'd been trying to do something a little romantic, which rarely included machetes and often included lobster.

"I didn't say you had to break me in gently," she

told him. "I just said I couldn't travel outside the US this first time."

"Fine. Next time, we can go someplace where there's a political coup happening during a tsunami."

"If there is a next time," she said.

Right. Because if her calculations were correct, and everything went according to plan, this would be the only time the two of them did this. For some reason the realization didn't sit well with Yeager. In spite of what he'd just said about political coups and tsunamis—as fun as that would have been—he already had their next time planned, and it would be a shame to have spent an entire week working on it for nothing. Hannah was going to love canyoneering in Morocco. Which reminded him…

"Just in case, did you apply for your passport?"

"Yes."

"And did you—"

"Yes, I paid the extra fee for expediting it," she answered before he could even put voice to the question. "I should have it in a couple of weeks."

"Good."

"If I need it."

Why was she harping on *if*? Was it such a hardship for her, sexing it up with him? Hell, she'd enjoyed that kiss as much as he had.

He decided to change the subject. "Ready to hike? We're burning daylight here."

He told himself he did not sound impatient. There

were still a lot of hours to fill before bedtime and the hike to their campsite would only use up a few. But that was okay. Just because Hannah wanted to wait until nightfall for the main event didn't mean they couldn't enjoy themselves before they enjoyed each other.

Six

It was dusk by the time Hannah and Yeager arrived at their campsite, made even duskier by the trees that towered overhead, obscuring what little was left of the sunlight. She was more than ready to call it a day. A walk in the park. Ha! Maybe if it was Yellowstone Park and the walk involved all eight billion acres of it. She'd figured hiking and walking were two different things, but she'd assumed those differences lay mostly in hiking being more vertical and walking being more horizontal. She now knew that hiking was actually different from walking in that it was like dousing your legs and feet in gasoline and then setting them on fire.

When they finally reached their destination, however, her mood improved considerably. Because, as the hiking path emptied into a clearing surrounded by evergreens that disappeared into a purpling sky, she saw a campsite setup that was more reminiscent of a vintage Hollywood epic than a modern epic adventure.

A round, canvas tent stood in the center, its flaps thrown back to reveal a platform bed with a pile of pillows. There was a copper chandelier with a dozen candles flickering in its sconces—the kind that worked on batteries, not the kind that could, left unattended, leave the Smoky Mountains in ashes—and a few others twinkled on a bedside table. To the right of the tent was a copper fire pit ready for lighting and a love seat laden with more pillows. On the other side was a table and chairs—set with fine china and crystal—and an oversize copper ice chest brimming with bottles and other containers. Across it all zigzagged strings of tiny white lights that glimmered like stars. Hannah had never seen a sight more dazzling.

"You didn't tell me we'd be glamping," she said with much delight.

"Glamping?" Yeager echoed dubiously.

When she turned to look at him, she could see he wasn't as charmed by the tableau as she was. In fact, the expression on his face probably would have been the same if he were staring at the stuff in the back of the butcher shop that never made it into the case.

"Yeah, glamping," she repeated. "Part glamour, part camping. I saw it on *Project Runway*."

"There is no glamour in camping," he stated decisively. "I mean, I didn't expect us to kill and clean our own dinner or sleep out in the open, but this…" He shook his head. "Adventure travel should never include throw pillows and wineglasses. I knew it was a bad idea to hire a company called Vampin' 'n' Campin'. There are way too many apostrophes in that name for it to be taken seriously. Unfortunately they were the only ones available on short notice."

"Well, I'm glad you did," she told him. "This is wonderful."

He made his way toward the site. Still sounding disgusted, he muttered, "The privy is probably copper-plated, too."

"There, see? We will, too, be roughing it," she said. "I've never spent a day of my life without plumbing or electricity." Although a couple of her foster homes had come close. She kept that to herself. No need to spoil the beauty of the moment. "And there's no tech out here. Talk about primitive conditions."

He made his way to the ice chest, withdrew a bottle to inspect its label, then grinned. "I guess this glamping thing has its upside. We won't have to drink our *Clos du Mesnil* warm. Now *that* would be roughing it."

Hannah joined him. "That ice isn't going to last three days," she said.

"No, but the solar-powered fridge and freezer they set up behind the tent will."

"Ah. Is the privy solar-powered, too?" she asked hopefully.

"It is. And compostable."

"And I think that's all I want to know about the plumbing. Unless," she added even more hopefully, "you also arranged for a solar-powered shower."

He chuckled. "It's not solar-powered, but there is a shower."

Considering the amount of sweating she'd done in the last few hours, Hannah definitely wanted to hear about that. "Okay, you can tell me about the shower."

"Actually, I can do better than that. I can show it to you."

She sighed. "That would be wonderful. I'd love to get clean before dinner."

"There should be some towels in the tent," he said. "Our bags should be in there, too. Grab whatever else you need."

When she entered the tent, she did, indeed, find their overnight bags, so she opened hers to collect some clean underwear, a red tank top and striped pajama bottoms, all of which would doubtless be a far cry from what Yeager's usual girlfriends wore for a night with him. But it was the best she could do on short notice and short funds. Not that she was

Yeager's girlfriend, so she couldn't be held to that standard, anyway. Even so, she was now wishing she'd had the foresight to cough up a few bucks for something that at least hinted at seduction. She tried to remind herself that she and Yeager weren't here for romance. But that didn't quite feel right, either.

She found the towels on a folding wooden chair, underneath a bar of soap and bottle of shampoo, both environmentally friendly. Hannah didn't care what Yeager thought about Vampin' 'n' Campin'. As far as she—a lover of the Great Indoors—was concerned, they did camping just fine.

She emerged from the tent to find him waiting for her near a break in the trees, looking almost otherworldly in the growing darkness. His black hair was silvered by the moonlight, his biceps strained against his T-shirt, and a shadow fell across his face, imbuing him with just enough of the sinister to send a ribbon of apprehension shimmying through her.

Was she really going to go through with this tonight? Could she? Even considering everything that was at stake, she was beginning to have her doubts. Yeager was just so…so… She battled a wave of apprehension. So intimidating. He was almost literally twice the man of any guy she'd ever dated. She normally went for guys who were born to be mild. The ones who carried a novel by some obscure author in their messenger bags and whose clothes were always adorably rumpled. Guys who spent the weekend working on their bicycles and whose dinner orders never included substitutions. Safe guys. Predictable guys. Uncomplicated guys. How was she going to react to guys like that after a few nights with Yeager? Especially if he would be popping in and out of her life *forever* once those nights were concluded?

Maybe she should go the sperm bank route. If she changed her mind right now and asked Yeager to take her back to New York tonight, she might still have time to get pregnant this month. Her baby's father would be anonymous and in no way a part of their lives. Then, someday, she'd meet a safe, predictable, uncomplicated guy she could have more children with. She and Safe Guy could spend the rest of their days raising their family among *Consumer Reports*–endorsed products in their picket-fenced, asbestos- and lead-free home that was landscaped with noninvasive, allergen-free plants, while they protected their children from perils like sugary breakfast cereal, dog breeds weighing more than seven pounds and team sports.

Yeah. That sounded like a *great* life. She couldn't *wait* to get started on that. Then she'd never have to suffer the heart-racing dangers of Yeager again.

"Did you forget something?" he asked when she made no move to join him.

Yeah. Her sense of self-preservation. But that was way too big to pack in an overnight bag.

"No, I think I'm ready."

Overstatement of the century.

He tilted his head toward the opening in the trees, so she forced her feet to move forward until she came to a halt beside him. Up close, he looked a little less sinister and a lot more seductive, so she decided—*oh, all right*—she could go through with having sex with him if she *had* to. She didn't want to waste a perfectly good ovulation, after all. At least, she hoped it was perfect.

Yeager eyed her thoughtfully for a few seconds and Hannah was torn between wishing she knew what he was thinking and hoping she never found out.

All he said, though, was, "It's this way." Then he preceded her down the path.

Oh, joy. More hiking.

The trees swallowed them up again, but Hannah didn't mind so much this time. With the sun down, the night was growing cooler and a gentle breeze rocked the leaves in the trees. Soft bursts of light erupted here and there, and it took her a moment to realize they were fireflies. She'd never seen even one, let alone the dozens that suddenly surrounded them, and she couldn't help the laughter that rippled from inside her.

"What's so funny?" Yeager asked, glancing over his shoulder.

"Fireflies," she said. "I've never seen them in person."

He stopped abruptly, turning to look at her. "You're joking."

She halted, too, since his big body blocked the path. "No, I'm not. I told you—I've never been out of New York."

"There are fireflies in New York," he said.

"Not in the neighborhoods where I've lived."

"You've never been outside the *City* of New York?" he asked incredulously. "I thought you meant the state."

She shook her head. "No, I meant the five boroughs."

He studied her in silence for a moment, but his face was in shadow again, so she couldn't tell what he was thinking. Finally he said, "What, one of the families you lived with couldn't even take you to Jones Beach for the day?"

In response Hannah only shrugged. Of course none of the families she'd lived with took her to Jones Beach. For most of them, she'd just been a way to add some money to their bank accounts. And for the few who had genuinely cared for the children they took in, all the money they received went to feed and clothe those children. There had never been anything left for luxuries like day trips.

"But you've seen the ocean, right?" Yeager asked. "Surely you hit Coney Island or Rockaway Beach at some point when you were a teenager."

"I didn't, actually," she confessed. "My friends

and I preferred prowling Manhattan whenever we had a little free time. And, truth be told, on those rare occasions I found myself with a little extra money to do stuff, I spent it on fabric instead."

He said nothing for another moment. "You've never seen the ocean?"

"No. I haven't. Or, if I did before I lost my mom, I don't remember it."

"How is that possible?"

Again she shrugged. Even as an adult freed from the confines of the foster care system, Hannah had never felt the need or desire to explore beyond the city. She just wasn't one to stray outside her comfort zone, even for small adventures. She liked knowing where she was and how to navigate her surroundings. The thought of taking a day trip someplace had just never appealed to her.

Yet here she was, hundreds of miles away from home—and for more than just a day—and she didn't feel unsettled at all. She hadn't even been nervous about boarding a plane or leaving New York. On the contrary, she'd been excited before they'd left, and she'd had a lot of fun today. Enough to make her think she should have tried something like this a long time ago.

But it was only because Yeager was with her, she told herself. He was familiar enough to her to offset the strangeness of this trip. She couldn't do this all the time, especially not alone. And, hey, she didn't *want* to do this all the time. Once she was settled back in New York, she'd return to being her usual complacent self again. She was sure of it.

Another sound suddenly joined the rustle of leaves overhead, drawing her attention away from her thoughts and back to the night surrounding them. Because even though this was her first time in the Great Outdoors, she recognized the sound. A waterfall. The shower Yeager had promised her was a waterfall. She'd assumed they were finished with adventures for the day—well, except for the greatest adventure of all that was still looming—yet here he was, presenting her with another. His life really was one exploit after another.

They exited the trees onto the banks of the river they'd navigated earlier, though here, it wasn't wide and rough with rapids. Here, it was narrow and flowed like silk. The waterfall was only about eight feet high, spilling into the river with a gentle percussion that sent ripples gliding outward. The sun had well and truly set by now, and the moon hung overhead like a bright silver dollar, surrounded by hundreds of glittering stars. Hannah had never seen the moon so bright and had never seen more than a few stars in the sky above her. She made her way carefully toward where Yeager had stopped on the edge of a rock, but she was so busy staring at the sky, she nearly walked right past him and into the river. He stopped her with a gentle hand to her shoulder, turning her until she faced him.

"Easy there, Sacagawea," he said. "The trail you're about to blaze could be your last."

She laughed, still looking at the sky. "I can't help it. It's so beautiful here."

"It's just your run-of-the-mill woods, Hannah."

Now she looked at Yeager. "It's not run-of-the-mill for me."

As she toed off her sneakers, she thought about how she must seem like an absolute freak to him. Her world was so tiny in comparison to his, her life experience virtually nonexistent. He lived for risk and danger, two things she wanted no part of. They couldn't be more different or less suited to each other. But that was good, right? It meant there was no chance of any messy emotional stuff getting in the way of their, ah, enterprise.

For a moment they only gazed at each other in silence. Well, except for the chirping of the crickets and the whisper of the wind and the shuffle of the waterfall. And, okay, the beating of Hannah's heart, which seemed to be loudest of all.

Yeager, however, seemed not to notice any of it, because he reached behind him and grabbed a handful of his T-shirt, pulling it over his head. "Come on," he said. "Last one in's a rotten egg."

Hannah scarcely heard what he said, because she was too busy staring at a half-naked Yeager. And even though she'd seen him half-naked a dozen times before, she'd never seen him as he was now—gilded by starlight and moonbeams and fireflies, looking like a creature of the night, if not the night itself. And then he was going to work on his fly, and she remembered he hadn't brought any clothes to change into after their swim—or even *for* their swim. And then she realized his half-naked state was about to become a full-naked state. And then... And then...

And then she was jumping into the river fully clothed, turning her back on him to feign much interest in the waterfall that was suddenly way more interesting than it should be, even for someone who'd never seen a waterfall in person before. The river was shallow enough here that she could stand with her head out of the water—just barely—but that didn't keep her knees from shaking. Though she was pretty sure that had nothing to do with the chill of the water. Especially since the water was surprisingly warm.

When she heard a splash behind her, she knew Yeager had joined her. And when she turned to see hiking boots and a pile of garments on the rock where he had been, she knew he was naked. She also knew that by the way he was grinning at her when he broke the surface of the water, jerking his head to sling back his wet hair.

And by his tone of voice when he said, "Most people undress before they bathe."

She bit back a strangled sound. "I just didn't want to be a rotten egg."

"Right."

"And I figured it might be a good idea to rinse out my clothes."

"Uh-huh."

"I mean, they did get pretty dirty today."

He swam toward her, quickly enough that Hannah, growing more panicky by the moment, didn't have a chance to swim away before he reached her.

"Well, then, let me help you," he said.

She felt his hands at the hem of her T-shirt and, before she could stop him, he was pushing it up over her torso. He took his time, though, opening his palms over her naked skin under the wet fabric, sliding his hands up over her waist and rib cage, halting just below her bra, the L of his index finger and thumb brushing the lower curves of her breasts. Her heart hammered even harder in her chest and heat pooled deep in her belly. His expression remained teasing, though, so she knew he was feeling none of the tumult she did.

"Lift your arms," he said softly.

Automatically she did and he tugged her shirt over her head, tossing it behind him toward the rock, where it landed perfectly alongside his own.

"Now the shorts," he said, moving his hand to the button at her waist.

Deftly, he undid it and the zipper, then tucked

his hands inside the garment, settling one on each of her hips. For a moment he only held her in place, the warmth of his palms permeating the cotton of her panties, a sensation that made the heat in her belly spiral outward, kindling fires in every part of her. Then he gripped her shorts and tugged them down, lifting first one leg then the other, until that piece of clothing, too, had been stripped from her and tossed to the riverbank.

Although she was still in her bra and panties, the equivalent of a bathing suit, the sensations coursing through her made Hannah feel like she was as naked as Yeager was. It didn't help that his teasing expression had gradually grown into something much more heated. And when he began to dip his head toward hers...

She quickly turned around and began swimming toward the waterfall with all her might. But she was no match for Yeager, who caught up to her immediately.

"There," he said as he drew up alongside her. "After that swim, everything you have on should be totally clean. Time to take it off."

Well, golly gee whiz. Nothing like getting right to it. Talk about a wham-bam-thank-you-ma'am.

"Are you always this pragmatic when it comes to sex?" she asked.

"I'm never pragmatic when it comes to sex," he assured her. "But I've never had sex on a timetable.

It's always a lot more spontaneous than this. And the reason for it is never baby-making. It's always merry-making."

"You don't think sex for making a baby can be fun?" she asked. "You just want to get this thing over with as quickly and cleanly as possible? Am I that unappealing to you?"

His response was to pull her close and cover her mouth with his, kissing her in a way that assured her he found her very appealing indeed, that he didn't intend for this thing to be in any way quick—never mind clean—and that he planned to have quite a lot of fun making a baby with her. By the time he pulled away from her, they were both breathing raggedly.

"Well, okay, then," Hannah managed to say.

But she still didn't take off her underwear. She just wasn't ready yet. It was a nice night. She was in a beautiful place with a beautiful man. She didn't feel the need to rush. So she turned onto her back to float on the water and look at the night sky. She heard Yeager emit a sound of reluctant resignation and then turn onto his back, too.

"Hey, that's the Big Dipper," she said, pointing toward a group of stars to the left of the moon. It kept her from looking at a naked Yeager floating on his back, gilded in moonlight.

"It is," he told her. "And you can follow the arc—"

"Follow the arc to Arcturus," she chorused with then finished for him. "I remember that from ninth-grade science. Isn't that weird? I don't think I remember anything else from that class. I'm not sure I even remember much from the rest of ninth grade. I moved around a lot in high school. Even more than when I was in elementary school."

He paddled closer to Hannah, so she paddled away. She really wasn't ready yet for a naked Yeager.

He growled restlessly, clearly frustrated that she was going to draw this out as long as she could. Despite that, he asked, "Where did you live when you were in ninth grade?"

"For the first three months, I was in Mott Haven," she told him. "Then they moved me to Vinegar Hill. After school broke for summer vacation, I went to Bed-Stuy for a while."

He was silent for a moment. Then softly he said, "You lived in some pretty rough neighborhoods."

"Yeah, well, you don't find too many people taking in foster kids on the Upper East Side. Go figure."

He was silent again.

"It wasn't all bad, Yeager," she told him. "I lived with a handful of families who were truly good people, and I still have friends I made while I was in the system. You only hear the horror stories about foster care in the news. But a lot of kids ended up way better off there than they were with their birth families."

"Did you ever wonder about your real family?"

"Sure. There were times when I would fantasize that someone must have made a mistake somewhere, and I really did have a mom and dad out there some-where. Like I was mistakenly switched with another baby at the hospital. Or the woman who died that they thought was my mom was actually misidentified and my mom was still out there in the world some-where, looking for me." She sighed. "But I knew it wasn't true. I knew I was right where I was supposed to be. It's just a weird irony that I actually wasn't."

"Sounds like little-kid Hannah was as down-to-earth as grown-up Hannah," Yeager said.

She didn't know whether to take that as a com-pliment or not. From his tone of voice, he seemed to respect down-to-earth people. On the other hand, he didn't spend much time in one place on the earth himself.

"How about you?" she asked, still gazing up at the sky. "Where were you in ninth grade?"

He hesitated for a telling moment. Then he said, so quietly that Hannah almost didn't hear him, "Peo-ria, Illinois."

His response surprised her enough that she forgot about his nakedness and glanced over at him. For-tunately—or not—it was dark enough now that the water had turned inky, hiding most of him. Of all the places she could have imagined Yeager being from, Peoria, Illinois, would never have made the cut.

"You actually grew up in the city that's an icon of Midwestern conservatism?"

"I actually did."

It occurred to her then how little she really knew of Yeager. Sure, he'd revealed snippets of his life from time to time during their conversations at Cathcart and Quinn, but she knew nothing about what had made him Yeager Novak, global adventurer. And suddenly, for some reason, she wanted to know that very badly.

"Did you live your whole life there?" she asked.

"I did until I was eighteen."

"What brought you to New York?"

"A full-ride hockey scholarship to Clarkson University in Potsdam."

"You play hockey?"

"I used to."

"What do your mom and dad do for a living?"

He sighed in a way that made her think he really, really, *really* didn't want to talk about this. Despite that, he replied, "My mom managed a bookstore and my dad was an accountant."

The son of a bookstore manager and an accountant had grown up to be one of the world's greatest risk-takers? How the hell had that happened?

"So how did you wind up—"

Before she could finish her question, he righted himself in the water and strode toward her. Hannah straightened, too. She thought he just wanted to get closer to continue their conversation. Instead, the moment he was within reaching distance, he wrapped an arm around her waist, pulled her toward him until she was flush against him and kissed her.

As he did, he reached behind her to unfasten her bra, slipping it over her arms and releasing it into the flow of the river. Hannah started to object at the loss of the garment, but Yeager moved his hands to her breasts, covering both with sure fingers, and anything she might have said got caught in her throat. He brushed the pad of one thumb over her sensitive nipple. When she gasped, he took advantage of her reaction to taste her more deeply. She opened her mouth wider to accommodate him, splaying one hand wide over the ropes of muscle on his torso, threading the fingers of the other through his silky, wet hair.

He growled something unintelligible against her mouth, then dragged soft, butterfly kisses along her jaw, her neck and her shoulder. The hand at her waist moved to her back, skimming until he gripped the wet cotton of her panties and pulled them down. Then he was caressing her naked bottom, curving his fingers over the swells of her soft flesh, guiding his fingers into its elegant cleft, penetrating her with the tip of one.

When Hannah cried out loud at the sensation, he moved again, pulling down her panties in the front to push his hand between her legs. She felt his fingers against her, moving through the folds of flesh made damp by her reaction to him, furrowing slowly at first, teasing her with gentle pressure. Hastily, she shed her panties completely, then opened her legs wider, silently inviting more. But instead of escalating his attentions, Yeager only continued with his slow and steady cadence, gliding his fingers over her until she felt as though she would burst into flame.

"Please, Yeager," she whispered. But those two words were the only ones she could manage.

He seemed to understand, though, because he slipped a finger closer to the feminine core of her, drawing languid circles before venturing inside. He entered her with one long finger, once, twice, three times, four, each with a single, long stroke to her clitoris that sent tremors of need shuddering through her. Before she could climax, though, he moved his hand away. She was about to beg him to touch her again, but he circled her wrist and guided her hand toward him instead, wrapping her fingers around his long length.

She opened her eyes to find him watching her intently, his blue eyes dark with wanting. So she enclosed his shaft at its base and stroked upward, curving her palm over its head before moving back down again. This time Yeager was the one to close his eyes, and this time it was his breath that hitched in his chest. When Hannah pulled her hand up and down him again, he reached for her, aligning her body against his, covering her mouth with his, tucking his hand between her legs once more.

For a long time they only kissed and caressed,

their gestures growing bolder and more invasive, until both were close to climax. Then Yeager lifted Hannah by her waist and wrapped her legs around his middle to enter her. Up and down he moved her body, going deeper inside her with every thrust. Gently he curved his hands under her bottom to lift her higher, bringing her down harder, entering her as deeply as he could.

The hot coil inside Hannah cinched tighter with every thrust, until she knew she was close to crashing. Then she felt his finger behind her again, pushing softly inside her, and she came apart at the seams.

Yeager held on for a few more moments then climaxed hard, spilling himself hot and deep inside her. He held her in place for a long time afterward, as if he wanted to ensure every drop of his essence found its way to her center.

Hannah lay her head against his shoulder and clung to him, shivering, though not from the soft circles of water eddying around them.

"Are you cold?" he whispered against her ear.

Somehow she managed to murmur, "No. I'm good."

She stopped herself before saying she was better than good, better than she'd ever been in her life, because she knew she must be imagining that. She'd just never had a lover like Yeager, that was all. He really was larger than life. A part of her was thrilled by that, but a part of her was sobered by it, too.

She might never have another experience—another adventure—like Yeager Novak again. And she just wasn't sure if that was a good thing or not.

Seven

Yeager was working in his office in the Flatiron Building, his tie loosened, the top two buttons of his dress shirt unfastened, when his assistant, Amira, texted him from her desk in End of the Earth's reception area. She only did that when she was trying to be discreet about something. In this case, it was that there was a Hannah Robinson, who didn't have an appointment, here to see him. Should she just show her the door the way she usually did with the women who came to see Yeager at the office without an appointment, or should she tell her to wait until he had a free moment, which would probably be in a couple of hours—maybe—and hope Hannah left on her own after sitting in the waiting room for a while?

Instead of texting back that she should do neither, Yeager headed out to the reception area himself and ignored Amira's astonished expression when he got there.

Hannah was standing with her back to him, studying an enlarged photo of the Sinabung volcano on Sumatra that he'd taken five years ago. The first thing he noticed was that her clothes matched the photo, her shirt the same rich blue as the sky, her skirt printed in the same variegated yellows as the sulfur. The second thing he noticed was that she didn't look pregnant.

He mentally slapped himself. Of course she didn't look pregnant. She could only be a couple of weeks along, at most, since it had only been eleven days since he'd last seen her and twelve since he'd made love to her. But she must be pregnant. Otherwise, why would she have come to his office? If their first effort had failed, she could have just texted him to say, *Sorry, see you next month.*

"Hey," he said by way of a greeting, his heart racing at the prospect of good news, way more than he expected it would in these circumstances.

She spun around, her gaze connecting immediately with his. That was when something cool and unpleasant settled in Yeager's midsection. Because he could tell by the look on her face that she *wasn't* pregnant.

"Come on back to my office," he said. Then, to

Amira, he added, "I'm unavailable for the rest of the morning. Maybe the afternoon, too."

"Sure thing, Yeager," Amira said, sounding even more shocked than she looked.

Hannah threw a soft but obviously manufactured smile at his assistant and murmured a quiet, "Thanks." Then she crossed her arms over her midsection and followed him silently to his office.

He closed the door behind them and directed her to one of two leather chairs in front of his massive Victorian desk. His office, like the rest of Ends of the Earth, was cluttered with antique furniture and vintage maps and artifacts. A deliberate effort to replicate a time when world travel was full of intrigue and danger, attempted by only the most intrepid explorers. He pulled the second chair closer to Hannah's and sat.

"It didn't work, did it?" he asked. "You're not pregnant, are you?"

She shook her head.

Even though he'd already known that was what she was going to say, he was surprised by the depth of his disappointment. He really had thought they'd be successful the first time they tried. They were healthy adults with even healthier libidos, and when they'd made love in North Carolina, it had been with exuberance and passion and a *very* long finish. In the days in between, they'd bungee jumped from an abandoned train trestle and zip-lined through the mountains. He still smiled when he remembered Hannah's expression and half-baked objections both times as he cinched her safety harness to his, followed by her unmitigated elation at the end of each adventure.

But his disappointment wasn't just for a failed effort after his confidence that they would succeed. He felt genuine sadness that there wasn't a tiny Yeager or Hannah growing inside her at this very moment. And it wasn't until now that he understood how very much he wanted to have this child with her.

"It's okay," he said. Even if it didn't really feel okay at the moment. "We'll try again."

Hannah nodded but she didn't look convinced. Not sure why he did it, Yeager lifted a hand and cupped her cheek in his palm. Then he leaned forward and pressed his lips lightly to hers. It was a quick, chaste kiss. One intended to reassure. But the moment his mouth touched hers, desire erupted inside him. It was all he could do not to swoop in for a second, more demanding kiss. Instead he dropped his hand to hers and wove their fingers together.

"Are you all right?" he asked.

Very softly she replied, "I think so."

He could tell she wanted to say more, but no other words came out. "Do you want to talk about it?" he asked.

"No," she said. Then she quickly amended, "Yes."

She expelled a frustrated sound. "I don't know. I feel so weird right now."

That made two of them.

"It's just…" She inhaled a deep breath and released it slowly, then met his gaze. Her beautiful silver-gray eyes seemed enormous and limitless, filled with something he had never seen in them before. Not just disappointment, but uncertainty. He'd never known Hannah to be a victim of either of those things. She was always so sunny and contented whenever he saw her. Even in her tiny apartment that offered so little to be sunny or contented with, she'd seemed to be both.

Hannah was one of those rare people who was satisfied with what life had brought her, even after life had brought her so little. Not that she didn't have aspirations or goals, but she wasn't blindsided by a single-minded, driven ambition that overshadowed everything else, the way most people were when they were going after what they wanted. She took life day by day and enjoyed what each of those days brought. At least, she had until now.

"It's not about the money, you know?" she said. "I mean, at first, it was. I did always plan on having kids someday, but my timetable was fluid where that was concerned, and I didn't really give it that much thought. Then, when I found out about my grandfather and all that money…" At this, she managed an almost earnest chuckle. "Well, hell, yeah, it was about the money. I could do everything I ever wanted if I inherited the Linden billions. But this morning, when I discovered I wasn't pregnant, it wasn't the money I thought about first. It was the baby. And how there wasn't going to be one. And I just felt so..."

She blinked and a single, fat tear spilled from one eye. Yeager brushed it away with the pad of his thumb before it even reached her cheek. Then he kissed her again. A little longer this time. Maybe because he needed reassuring as much as she did, which was the most surprising thing of all this morning.

"It's okay," he repeated. "I bet no one gets pregnant the first time they try." He smiled gently. "Really, when you think about all the logistics that go into procreating, it's amazing anyone ever gets pregnant at all."

He had meant for the comment to lighten the mood. Instead, Hannah looked horrified.

"I'm kidding," he said quickly. "It'll happen, Hannah. Don't worry. This just gives us the chance to go to Malta next time. I know this very isolated, extremely wild beach where there are some incredible caves for diving. You'll love it. I promise. A few days in the Mediterranean, lying on a sunny beach, eating all that great food..." He stopped himself from adding the part about the virile young stud she'd be spending her nights with, since that part went without saying. "Who wouldn't get pregnant with all that as a backdrop?"

She smiled again and, this time, it was a little more convincing. "You're taking me to the beach," she said.

"I am."

"I'll finally get to see the ocean."

"You will."

"How long have you been planning this trip?"

Yeager had started planning it in North Carolina, the minute she'd told him she'd never seen the ocean. For some reason, though, he didn't want to admit that. So he hedged. "I've had a few ideas for destinations in my head all along. Malta was just one of them."

Which was true. He just didn't mention that Malta had been at the bottom of the list, since beaches, even the Mediterranean ones, were usually pretty lacking in adventure, and besides, when you've seen one beach and ocean, you've pretty much seen them all. Except, of course, for Hannah. So Malta it was.

"That's sweet of you, Yeager."

It wasn't sweet of him. He just didn't think it was fair that a perfectly nice person like Hannah had never seen the ocean, that was all. And, hey, that Mediterranean diet was supposed to be all kinds of healthy.

"Will it be a problem for you to take the time off from work?" he asked.

"I'm sure Mr. Cathcart and Mr. Quinn won't be too crazy about me asking off again. But when I remind them how, in the ten years I've worked for them, I hadn't had a single vacation before last month, they'll probably grudgingly concede. I'm not sure how many more times I'll be able to play that card, though. And it really will eat into my paycheck."

Yeager started to offer to intercede on her behalf with her employers for her again and cover any of her lost wages. Then he remembered how adamant Hannah had been that she could make her own way. Besides, he really was sure the trip to Malta would be, ah, fruitful. There was a good chance Hannah wouldn't need to ask for any more time off, because she'd be able to quit that job and follow her dreams.

"It'll be okay, Hannah," he told her a third time. Because three was a charm, right?

Except in baby-making, he quickly amended. In baby-making, two was. They *would* be successful next time. Yeager was sure of it.

Hannah stood on the balcony of the breathtaking suite in the luxury hotel Yeager had booked for them in Valletta, gazing out at the Grand Harbour at night, waiting for him to finish his shower.

She was beginning to understand why he lived the way he did. This place was amazing. The city was awash with light against the black sky, practically glowing with a golden grandeur reflected in the water of the bay. The moon and stars, too, were gilded with an otherworldly radiance that made her feel as if she'd completely left the planet and arrived on some ethereal plane. She couldn't be farther removed from her life in New York than she would be if she were standing at the outer reaches of the universe.

The mere view from a European balcony wasn't enough to satisfy Yeager's idea of adventure, though. For him, the adventure for this trip had lain in the ocean caves where they'd spent yesterday diving. And that had certainly been fun. But to Hannah, the true adventure was simply being in a place that was so different from her own. There really was a lot more to the world than the neighborhoods she'd called home. And she'd only visited two places at this point. Maybe, if everything worked out the way it was supposed to, once her life settled down, she'd think about doing a little more globe-trotting with her child or children in the future.

A wave of apprehension spilled over her. Right now, that *child or children* was still a big *if*. Though she and Yeager were spending this trip at a more leisurely pace than their days in North Carolina. The cave diving yesterday had been peaceful—even the heart-racing moments of interacting with a real, live, albeit small, octopus—and today, they'd lain in the sun and strolled along the streets of Valletta and stuffed themselves with local cuisine. With any luck, Hannah would drop an egg at some point tomorrow—or the next day—that was ripe for fertilization. And tonight…

The thought stopped there. Yeah. Tonight. Tonight was… Tonight would be… She sighed. This time last month she'd been looking at the night ahead as a task necessary for her to complete to claim her legacy. Not that she hadn't liked the idea of having sex with Yeager—a lot—but, originally, that was all it was supposed to be: sex with Yeager. Something that would conveniently lead to her achieving her goal of starting a family. After actually having sex with Yeager, however, everything seemed to…shift. She still couldn't put her finger on what was different about this attempt to become pregnant from the last one, but there was definitely something. Something different about Yeager. Something different about her.

When she heard a door open in the suite behind her, she spun around to see him emerging from the bathroom wearing nothing but a pair of midnight blue boxers, scrubbing his black hair dry with a towel.

She watched as he crossed to the walk-in closet and stepped inside it. He then withdrew, wearing buff-colored trousers and buttoning up a chocolate-brown shirt. She recognized both as pieces she had made for him, and a ribbon of unexpected pleasure wound through her. She didn't know why. She'd probably made, or at least altered, half his wardrobe, the same way she had for many of Cathcart and Quinn's clients. His wearing of her clothes had never affected her any more than some other man's wearing of them. For some reason, though, she suddenly liked the idea of Yeager being wrapped in garments she had sewed for him.

She continued to watch him as he strode to a table where a bottle of champagne had been chilling since they'd returned from their day in town. Deftly, he popped the cork and poured two flutes, then nestled the bottle back into the ice. Hannah didn't think she could ever get tired of just looking at him. He moved with such ease and elegance, utterly assured in himself but completely unconscious of that confidence. She remembered how, in North Carolina, he'd revealed his seemingly quiet upbringing in the heart of the Midwest. Try as she might, he hadn't let her bring up the subject again. And she was dying to know how that little boy from Peoria had become such a raging scion of world adventure.

He made his way toward the French doors leading to the balcony, where Hannah awaited him in the darkness. His eyes must not have adjusted from the light of the room because he didn't seem to see her at first. Then he smiled and headed toward her. He halted just before reaching her, though, and gave her a thorough once-over.

"Wow," he said. "You look incredible."

She warmed at the compliment. They had reservations for a late dinner at some upscale seafood place he'd told her was one of his favorite places in the world. She'd had to scramble to find something to bring with her that would be suitable, since *upscale* didn't exist in her normal wardrobe—or her normal life, for that matter. Fortunately she'd had a couple of large enough fabric remnants to stitch together a flowy, pale yellow halter dress and had found some reasonably decent dressy sandals at her favorite thrift shop.

She was also wearing the strapless bra and brief panties Yeager had given her their first day in Valletta to compensate for the ones he'd sent down the river in North Carolina. Or so he'd said. Somehow, though, the sheer ivory silk-and-lace confections bore no resemblance to the cotton Hanes Her Way that they'd replaced. And she was reasonably certain they didn't come in two- and five-packs.

"Thanks," she said, the word coming out more quietly and less confidently than she'd intended. "You look pretty amazing yourself."

He smiled. "Thanks to you."

Another frisson of delight shuddered through her. Why was his opinion suddenly more important to her than it had been before? She knew she was good at her job—she didn't need the approval of others to reinforce that. But Yeager's approval suddenly meant a lot to her.

He handed her a glass of champagne then turned to look at the city lights she'd been marveling at. "I think this may be one of the most beautiful cities I've ever visited," he said.

There was a wistfulness in his voice she'd never heard before. She wouldn't have thought Yeager Novak could be wistful. She smiled. "You talk like there are actually cities you haven't visited."

He chuckled. "One or two."

She shook her head. "I can't imagine living the life you do. Are you ever in one place for any length of time?"

"I try to spend at least one week a month in New York," he said.

"One week is not a length of time," she told him.

"Maybe not to you. But even a week in one place can make me restless. Besides, I can pretty much run Ends of the Earth from anywhere. And there are times when I have to be out of the country for months."

"Have to be?" she echoed. "Or just want to be?"

He lifted one shoulder and let it drop. "Could be they're one and the same."

Interesting way to put it.

"So, what?" she asked. "You just live in hotels?"

"Sometimes. Or in tents. Or out in the open. Depends on where I am. I do own homes in the places I visit most often."

"Which are?"

He turned to look at her full-on. "I don't want to talk about me. Let's talk about you."

She shook her head adamantly. "Oh, no. No way. We talked about me the whole time in North Carolina. You know everything there is to know about me. This time, we're going to talk *aaalll* about you."

He bristled palpably at the comment. Hannah didn't care. The last time they were together, he'd avoided every effort she'd made to learn more about him, always turning the conversation back to her.

Yeager really did know everything there was to know about her. About how she'd nearly failed phys ed at her Harlem middle school because she was so bad at gymnastics. About the four stitches and tetanus shot she'd had to get when she was seven, after slicing open her knee in a vacant lot on Lexington Avenue. About how, to this day, she still missed the grumpy, one-eyed tabby named Bing Clawsby that had lived in one of her homes.

He knew her favorite color was purple, her favorite food was fettuccine Alfredo, her favorite movie was *Wall-E* and her favorite band was the Shins. He knew she was a Sagittarius, that she'd never learned how to drive, that she believed in ghosts and, how, if she could be any animal in the world, she'd be a fennec fox. All she knew about him was that he was the only child of a quiet-sounding couple from Peoria and that he'd played hockey for a college so far upstate he might as well have been in Canada. He wasn't going to avoid her this time.

"Oh, come on," she said. "How bad can your secrets be? You barely have two thousand hits on Google."

He arched his eyebrows at that. "You looked me up online?"

"Of course I looked you up online." Hell, she'd done it after the first time he'd come into Cathcart and Quinn. There was no reason he had to know that part, though. "You're going to be the father of my child." She hoped. "But all that turned up was your social media accounts, stuff about Ends of the Earth, and mentions in some extreme adventure blogs. Even that article about you in *Outside* magazine didn't reveal anything about the real Yeager Novak."

He enjoyed a healthy taste of his champagne and avoided her gaze. Hannah remained silent as she waited him out. She was surprised when she won the battle after a few seconds and he turned to gaze out at the bay again.

Quietly he said, "That article in *Outside* revealed everything you need to know about me."

"It didn't tell me you're from Peoria."

"That's because Peoria isn't a part of my life."

"But it's where you grew up," she objected. "Where and how a person grows up is a huge part of who they are."

"It's a huge part of who they *were*," he argued. "You can't go home again."

"Everyone goes home again at some point, Yeager, in some way. It's inescapable." When he said nothing she asked, "Do your folks still live in Peoria?"

He sighed that sigh of resignation she was beginning to recognize fairly well. "No," he told her. "They died within a year of each other when I was in college."

"Oh," she said soberly. "I'm sorry."

She was sorry for his loss, not sorry that she'd asked. This was exactly the sort of thing two people should be sharing when their lives were going to be linked—she hoped—by a child. The things that had impacted them, the things that had shaped and moved them.

"I was one of those late-life surprises," he said. "My mother was fifty-two when I was born. My father was nearly sixty. He had a fatal heart attack my junior year of college. My mom had a stroke ten months later."

Which could explain one of the reasons Yeager kept himself so physically fit. It didn't, however, explain why he kept traversing the globe over and over.

"I'm sorry," Hannah said again.

He gazed down into his glass. "It was a long time ago."

Maybe. But two losses like that, so close together,

had to have taken a toll on a college kid hundreds of miles away from home.

Hannah changed the subject from his parents to his school. "So…hockey scholarship. You must have been pretty good."

He nodded. "I was, actually. I had interest from a couple of pro teams before I graduated."

"Why didn't you stay with it?"

He shrugged again, even more half-heartedly. "Hockey was something I shared with my dad. He was my coach when I started in a youth league at five. He took me to Blackhawk games once a month before I even started school, even though Chicago was a three- or four-hour drive one-way. We'd make a weekend of it—my mom would come, too—and we'd do touristy stuff while we were there. Hit Navy Pier or the Shedd Aquarium or the Field Museum or something. And my dad never missed one of my games, all the way through high school. He even hung around the rink to watch me practice when he could. After he died, it wasn't the same. Hockey didn't mean as much to me as it did before. I just didn't have the heart for it anymore, you know?"

Hannah didn't know, actually. She could no more imagine what that had been like for Yeager than she could swim from here to New York. She'd never had a relationship like that—had never shared anything like that—with anyone. So she didn't respond.

He didn't seem to expect an answer, anyway, because he continued. "That was when Tommy and I started talking about going into business together. He'd spent his childhood living all over the world, thanks to his mom's job, and after my parents' deaths, going someplace else in the world—anywhere else in the world—sounded pretty damned good to me. So that was where we put our efforts."

Hannah had thought it would take the entirety of their trip this time—and then some—to uncover what it was that made Yeager tick. But in less time than it took to drink a glass of champagne, she was beginning to understand exactly why he'd become the traveler and risk-taker he was. It was clear he'd been very close to his parents, and that they'd been a loving family. A family he'd lost while he was still a kid and whom he missed terribly. A part of him might even still be looking for that family, in his own way.

Maybe, deep down, she and Yeager weren't quite so different as she'd first thought. But where her way to deal with that loss was to stay put in one place to try to a build a life there, his was to escape any reminder of what he'd once had.

He lifted his glass, drained its contents, then gazed at the bay again. Hannah sipped her champagne carefully—the way she did everything—and studied him in silence. After a moment he almost physically shook off his sober mood and looked at her again. He even smiled. Kind of.

Evidently heartened by having overcome the most difficult hurdle she could throw in front of him, he asked, "So what else do you want to know about me?"

She smiled back. "Favorite color?" Even though she already knew it was blue.

"Blue."

"Favorite food?"

"Anything from the ocean that's been blackened and grilled."

And on it went until she knew his favorite movie was *High Noon* and his favorite band was whatever happened to be streaming that didn't suck. That he was, ironically, a Virgo. That he even knew how to drive—and actually preferred—a stick shift. That he thought ghosts were a lot of hooey and that, of all the animals in the world, he'd choose to be not a lone wolf but a Komodo dragon because, hey, dragon.

By the time Hannah finished her interrogation, Yeager was pouring the last of the champagne into their glasses, and she was feeling mellower than she'd ever felt in her life. In North Carolina, they'd scarcely had a single minute when they weren't doing something adventurous. Including the sex, which, even though they'd had a perfectly good bed in their glamping tent, had happened that last time on a blanket in a clearing in the woods, under the stars, surrounded by fireflies. They'd been stargazing at the time, then one thing had led to another and, suddenly, Hannah had been naked, and then Yeager had been naked, and then she'd been on all fours with him behind her, thrusting into her again and again and again, and, well... It had just been, you know, super, super adventurous the whole time.

Anyway.

This time felt a lot less demanding. A lot less needful. A lot less urgent.

Until she looked at Yeager again and realized that, somehow, he was thinking about the exact same things she'd just been thinking about. Right down to the nakedness, the all fours and the thrusting again and again and again.

"You know," he said softly, "we can always cancel our dinner reservation."

Heat erupted in Hannah's belly at the suggestion. "But I thought you said it was one of your favorite places to eat in the whole, wide world."

His gaze turned incandescent. "I can think of other places I like better."

"How do you always know what I'm thinking?" she asked, her voice scarcely a whisper.

"I don't," he told her. "Except when you're thinking about sex. It's your eyes. They get darker. And there's something there that's just...wild. You have the most expressive eyes I've ever seen in a human being. At least, they are when it comes to wanting something."

"Or someone," she said before she could stop herself.

He took her glass from her hand and set it with his on the balcony railing. "We should definitely cancel our dinner reservation," he said decisively.

"Okay," Hannah agreed readily. Although she was certainly hungry, dinner was the last thing on her mind. "If we *have* to."

Yeager took her hand in his and tugged her to him. Then he dipped his head and kissed her. It was a gentle kiss, with none of the heat and urgency she knew was surging through both of them. He brushed his lips over hers, once, twice, three times, four, then covered her mouth completely with his, tasting her long and hard and deep.

Oh. Okay. There was the heat. There was the urgency. There was the…

He skimmed one hand over her bare shoulder and down her arm, settling it on her waist to pull her closer.

Hannah went willingly, looping her arms around his neck, tangling the fingers of one hand in his still-damp hair. His heat surrounded her, pulling her into him, until she wasn't sure where her body ended and his began. Slowly he began moving them backward, into their suite. He paused long enough to switch off the single lamp that had been illuminated, and then they were bathed in the pale light of the moon and the golden city outside.

Yeager continued to kiss her as he guided them toward the bed, his tongue tangling with hers, his mouth hot against her skin. He reached for the tie of her halter at the same moment she reached for the button of his trousers. As she unzipped his pants, he unzipped her dress, until the garment fell into a pool around her feet. She felt his member surge against her fingers, hard and heavy against the soft silk of his boxers. So she tucked her hand inside to cover him, bare skin to bare skin. He was so... *Oh.* And she could scarcely wait to have him inside her again.

As she stroked him, he bent his head and tasted her breast over the fabric of her bra, laving her with the flat of his tongue until her nipple strained against the damp fabric. His hand at her waist crept lower, his fingers dipping into the waistband of her panties, then lower still, between her legs. Somehow, Hannah managed to take a small step to the side to open herself wider to him, and he threaded his fingers into the damp folds of her flesh. She gasped at the contact, gripping his shoulder tight when her legs threatened to buckle beneath her, her caressing of his erection growing slower and more irregular.

Yeager didn't seem to mind. As he fingered her with one hand, he moved the other to her back, expertly unfastening her bra until it fell to the floor, too. Then he pulled as much of her breast as he could into his mouth, the pressure of his tongue against her nipple coupled with his hand between her legs bringing her near orgasm. When he realized how close she was, he moved his hand away, dragging his wet fingers up over her torso to cradle her breast in his palm.

He lifted his head again and covered her mouth with his, kissing her deeply. His member twitched beneath her hand, and she knew a keen desire to have him inside her *now*. With trembling fingers, she freed him long enough to unbutton his shirt and shove it from his shoulders. Then she tugged his trousers and his boxers down over his hips, kneeling before him to skim them off his legs completely. When he stood in front of her, towering over her, his member straight and stiff, Hannah couldn't help herself. She wrapped her fingers around him and guided him toward her mouth.

He groaned his approval at her gesture, tangling his fingers in her hair. She ran her tongue down the length of him, back up again, then covered the head of his shaft completely, pulling him deep inside. Eagerly, she consumed him, taking her time to pleasure them both until she knew he was close to his breaking point. Only then did she rise again, dragging her fingers up along his thighs and taut buttocks, over the ropes of sinew and muscle on his torso, pushing herself up on tiptoe to kiss him as hungrily as he had her.

He reached for her panties and pushed them down over her hips, and she pulled them the rest of the way off. Then he lifted her up off the floor and, after one more fierce kiss, threw her playfully to the center of the bed. She landed on her fanny with a laugh, until he joined her, spreading her legs wide to bury his head between them.

Now Hannah was the one to gasp—and moan and purr—as he devoured her, drawing circles with the tip of his tongue, nibbling the sensitive nub of her clitoris until she thought she would come apart at the seams. Then he was turning their bodies so that he was sitting on the edge of the mattress again, with her astride him, facing him. Gripping her hips, he lowered her over his shaft, bucking his hips upward as he entered her, long and hard and deep. Hannah did cry out then, so filled was she by him. He moved her up, then down, then up again, until she picked up his rhythm fluently. Over and over their bodies joined, until they seemed to become one. And then they were climaxing together, Yeager surging hotly inside her.

Immediately he turned them again, so that Hannah was on her back and he was atop her, bracing himself on his strong forearms. He murmured something about staying inside her until he was sure she was pregnant this time—because he was sure she would be pregnant this time—then kissed her again for a very long time.

All Hannah could do was open her hands over the hot, slick skin of his back and return the kiss, and hope like hell he was right.

Eight

It was raining in New York the second time Hannah came to see Yeager at his office. Since undertaking this…this…this whatever it was with her—since *deal* didn't seem like the right word anymore—he'd been trying to stay close to his home base as much as he could. That way, when Hannah had good news to tell him, she could do so in person.

But he knew the moment she stepped into his office—he'd told Amira weeks ago to send Hannah back anytime she showed up—that she didn't have good news. Her dark expression was completely at odds with the bright pink-and-orange dress she was wearing, and she didn't look as if she'd slept for days.

Something cold and unpleasant settled in Yeager's midsection. He'd been disappointed last month when she'd told him she wasn't pregnant, but this… What he was feeling now went beyond disappointment. It went beyond sadness. He wasn't even sure there was a word to cover the emotions swirling inside him at the moment.

Hannah, though, looked even worse than he felt. So he rose and rounded his desk, ushering her to the same chair she'd sat in before, drawing his up alongside hers. As he had before, he took her hand in his and wove their fingers together.

And he did his best to inject a lightness he didn't feel into his voice when he said, "Another miss, huh?"

She nodded silently.

"It's okay, Hannah," he told her, just as he had the first time. And, just like the first time, it didn't feel okay at all. "There's still plenty of time before the deadline." Even though he sincerely doubted it was the deadline she was worrying about right now.

Her reply was a heavy sigh, followed by a soft, "I know."

Still forcing his cheerfulness, trying not to choke on it, he added, "And, hey, bonus, we'll get to spend more time together."

It wasn't until he said it that he realized that actually would be a bonus. He'd enjoyed his two trips with Hannah more than he'd thought he would. He liked being around her. She brought an aspect to his travels he'd never had before—the newness of the experience. He'd forgotten how much fun going someplace for the first time could be. Hell, he couldn't even remember the last time he'd gone someplace for the first time. Watching Hannah's exuberance rafting down the Chattanooga River and seeing her euphoria in the underwater caves of Gozo, he'd felt like he was seeing it all for the first time, too.

He supposed, in a way, he had been. Because he didn't think he'd ever approached adventuring the way she did. For Yeager, going someplace else in the world felt like an escape. Hell, it was an escape. For Hannah, it was a discovery. Which, maybe, was what an adventure was supposed to be about in the first place.

He pushed the thought away. He pushed all his thoughts away and focused on Hannah. He hadn't been lying when he'd said she had the most expressive eyes he'd ever seen on a human being. He had been lying when he'd told her they were only expressive when it came to sex. He'd said that in Malta because he'd wanted sex at the moment, and so had she, and it had been the perfect segue to it—not that either of them had really needed one. Her eyes really were the proverbial window onto her soul. He always knew what Hannah was thinking lately, no matter what she was thinking about. Just by looking into her eyes.

And what she was thinking now was that she was

never going to get pregnant. Yeager begged to differ. They'd tried twice. Big damn deal. He knew people who had tried for years to get pregnant, then had two or three rug rats in a row. Not that he and Hannah had years—although, he had to admit, the idea of that wasn't as off-putting to him as it might have been a couple of months ago—but they did still have time. The clock on her inheritance had started ticking in July. That meant she had until January to get pregnant. It was only October. Including this month, they had three more shots. So to speak. Was it crazy that Yeager was suddenly kind of hoping they'd have to use up them all?

Hannah still hadn't replied to his last comment about how getting to spend more time together would be a bonus. Maybe she didn't think of it that way. Maybe what no longer felt like a deal to him was still very much a deal to her. Maybe she wasn't enjoying this as much as he was. Maybe she was just going through the motions and—

Yeah, right. As though the way the two of them had come together in Valletta, and before that, in North Carolina, was going through the motions. Hannah Robinson might be circumspect and careful when it came to living her life, but when it came to sex, she'd been surprisingly, gratifyingly adventurous.

An idea suddenly struck him. "Hey," he said, "if

you could go anywhere in the world you wanted, where would you go?"

She gazed at him questioningly. "What do you mean?"

"I mean the two trips we've taken so far have been ones I've put together. I'd still like to honor Tommy's spirit and leave my legacy through an adventure, but maybe the secret to this baby-making is to go someplace *you* want to go. Do something *you* want to do. What do you think?"

Although the question seemed to stump her, it also seemed to pull her out of her funk. "I don't know," she said. "I've never really thought about it." Then she braved a soft smile. "Jones Beach?"

He smiled back. But there was no way he was going to let her get away with a day trip she could take anytime she wanted to when he could take her anywhere in the world.

"Come on," he coaxed. "When you were a kid, there had to be someplace you dreamed about going. Something you dreamed about doing."

"Yeager, I've spent my whole life imagining being able to *stay* in one place and *not* move around."

He didn't buy it. "There's not a kid in the world who hasn't wanted to go someplace far away at some point and do something they've never done before. Think about it for a minute."

For a minute, she did. Then she smiled again. A

better smile this time. One that did something to Yeager's insides he'd never felt before. Weird.

"Okay, so when I was about six or seven," she said, "I read this book. *Stellaluna*. Are you familiar with it?"

He shook his head. He'd never been a huge reader growing up and what little reading he had done was always about sports or superheroes.

She continued. "It's about a baby fruit bat named Stellaluna who gets separated from her mother and is taken in by a family of birds. She has to live by the birds' rules, which are totally counter to her own bat instincts, but they become a family. All the while, though, Stellaluna's mother is looking for her. In the end, she finds her and they live happily ever after. So you can see why I read the book a million times when I was a kid and why I identified so much with a fruit bat."

"I can absolutely see that," Yeager agreed. And he absolutely could.

"For a while," she went on, "I got onto this fruit bat kick. I read a lot about them, and I decided that, even though the book never mentions where Stellaluna lives, she lived in a rainforest in Madagascar. And I thought Madagascar sounded like a really cool place."

"So you want to go to Madagascar," he said.

Hannah nodded. "Either that or Hogwarts."

He laughed. He was still disappointed that Hannah wasn't pregnant. But there was something about the prospect of trying again that made him feel better. He told himself it was because he hadn't been to Madagascar for a long time. But it was probably more because, this time, he'd be seeing it with Hannah.

"I can't help you with Hogwarts," he said. "But we can definitely go to Madagascar. Did you know there are treehouses there that you can rent?"

At this, Hannah lit up in a way he hadn't seen from her in months. Not since that night in North Carolina when she'd seen her first fireflies.

"We could really live like Stellaluna?" she asked.

"Yeah."

And if living out her childhood dream didn't put Hannah in the family way, Yeager didn't know what would.

Then another thought struck him. "Will it be a problem to take time off from work again?"

She sighed. "Yeah. But I'll handle it. I may have to finally explain to Mr. Cathcart and Mr. Quinn about my grandfather's will, which was something I really didn't want to share with anyone until I got pregnant, since I may nev—"

"Yes, you will," Yeager cut her off. And before she could say anything else, he added, "I'll have Amira clear my morning. You and I can make the plans together."

The light in Hannah dimmed some at that. "I can't," she said. "I have to be at work in a half hour."

"Right," he said. "But you have an hour for lunch, don't you?"

She nodded.

"So I'll meet you at one at Cathcart and Quinn. I'll bring lunch and my tablet with me. We'll make the arrangements then."

"Are you sure you have the time for all that?"

Was she nuts? Yeager Novak not have time for the mother of his offspring?

"Of course I have time. I'll see you at one."

"Okay."

"A Madagascar treehouse, Hannah. That will do the trick," he promised her. "This time next month, you'll be pregnant. I'm sure of it."

But the Madagascar treehouse didn't do the trick. And neither did the isolated castle in Scotland—the closest thing Yeager and Hannah could find to Hogwarts—in November. By the middle of December, she was so convinced there was something wrong that made it impossible for them to conceive that they both had their doctors do a second workup to see if that was the case.

But the results were the same then as they'd been in the summer, before they'd even started trying to conceive—they were both healthy, fertile adults for whom conception should pose no problem. Hannah's doctor tried to reassure her that it was perfectly normal for some couples to take several months to conceive and that, sometimes, the harder two people tried, the more elusive conception became. "Relax," her doctor told her. "Don't worry about it. It will happen."

Which was all well and good, Hannah thought a few evenings later in her apartment, if there weren't other factors at play. Billions of factors, in fact. If she wasn't able to inherit the Linden family fortune—her family fortune—she could be working for the rest of her life at a job that barely enabled her to take care of herself, never mind a child. Her fifty thousand dollar consolation prize would make the start of a nice nest egg, but it wasn't enough to start a business and keep it going here in New York. And without the funds to get Joey & Kit off the ground, there was no way she would ever be able to support a family. Yes, she might someday meet Mr. Right and get married and settle down. With two incomes coming in, she might be able to launch Joey & Kit and eventually turn it into a viable business.

Then again, she might not do any of those things. Nothing in life was guaranteed. Unless maybe you had billions of dollars.

And with or without the Linden fortune, Hannah knew now without question that she wanted to start a family. That had become clearer every time a pregnancy test came back negative and she was overcome by a sadness unlike any she'd ever known. Finding her Mr. Right would be beneficial in more than just a financial sense. But finding him was going to become more and more difficult the more time she spent with Yeager. The last five months with him had been the most enjoyable she'd ever spent. And not just because of the travels and adventures, either.

With every moment she spent with him, he crept further under her skin. She wasn't sure she'd ever be able to forget him once their time together came to an end—with or without a child. Before going into this venture with him, she'd considered him a frivolous, one-dimensional player. A guy who was fun to talk to and easy on the eyes, but who could never take anything in life seriously—especially a woman or a family. But she knew now that wasn't true. Yeager Novak was… He was…

She gazed out the only window in her apartment, at the back of the building on the next block. During the warm months, the backyards and fire escapes of both that building and hers were alive with activity, from Mr. Aizawa's tending of his bonsai trees to Mrs. Medina's courtyard flamenco lessons to the luscious smells wafting over from the Singhs' rooftop tandoor. In December, though, everything was still and quiet. Christmas lights twinkled from the Blomqvists' balcony, the Gorskis had lit the first candle in their window menorah and Lilah Windermere was revving up for Saturnalia, her share of the fire escape bedecked with suns and crescent moons.

Yeager Novak, Hannah continued with her thoughts, was the sort of man a woman could easily—oh, so easily—fall in love with. There was just something inside him that connected with something inside her—she didn't know any other way to put it. He was kind and smart and funny. And, for the last couple of months, he'd put her needs before his own.

She had always thought his incessant travels were due to some misplaced desire to prove he could live forever. He'd said as much himself, both that first night when he'd turned down her offer to father her child, and again the evening he'd agreed to. Now she understood, even if Yeager didn't, that he moved around so much to escape the loneliness of having lost his family when he was young. There were times when she even wondered if his agreement to donate a second set of chromosomes for her child might be the result not of his wish for a legacy, but of an unconscious desire to recreate the family he no longer had.

He was a good man. A complicated man. A multilayered man. A man with more substance and appeal than anyone she knew. Not the kind of guy Hannah normally went for at all. Which, maybe, was why she was falling for him so much harder.

The buzz of her doorbell interrupted her thoughts and she was grateful. She somehow knew before she even crossed to the intercom and heard his voice that it would be Yeager. But she didn't know why he'd be dropping by on a wintry Wednesday evening. They weren't supposed to meet again until Saturday morning, New York time, when they would arrive separately in Fiji for their final adventure together—this one to camp near a volcano on Koro Island. Yeager had read it was the site of an ancient fertility ritual and he intended to recreate it, right down to the running naked across hot coals after ingesting copious amounts of kava from a coconut shell. He had to leave tomorrow for a trip to Vancouver, but would take a red-eye to Suva and meet her within an hour of her own arrival.

A few months ago Hannah would have been excited by the idea of an adventure in Fiji, especially with Yeager. Tonight the thought of another quick trip—the most exotic one of all—only to return to her normal life a week later held no appeal. Her normal life, period, didn't hold much appeal these days. Which was, perhaps, the most troubling realization of all. Even if it hadn't been remarkable, her life five months ago had been perfectly acceptable to her. Then Gus Fiver of Tarrant, Fiver & Twigg walked in and everything—*everything*—changed. She wondered now if she would ever be content again.

She buzzed Yeager in and opened her front door, meeting him at the top of the stairs. He was still dressed for work, in a tailored, black wool coat flapping open over a charcoal suit—though he'd unbuttoned his shirt collar and loosened his tie. Hannah, too, was still in her work clothes, a black pencil skirt paired with a red sweater and red-and-black polka-dot tights.

As he topped the last stair, she started to take a step back toward her apartment to give him room. Before she could, though, he swept her up against him and dropped a swift kiss on her lips. The gesture surprised her. Especially when, after he completed it, he made no move to release her.

Instead he gazed into her eyes and murmured, "Hi. How you doing?"

"I… I'm good," she stammered. And then, because she couldn't think of anything else to say, thanks to the way the blood zipping through her veins made her a little—okay, a lot—muddleheaded, she added, "How are you?"

He grinned. "I'm good, too. I thought maybe we could do something tonight."

Her eyebrows shot up at that. "Why?"

He chuckled. "Why not?"

"Because I'm not… I mean, it's not time for me to… I still have a couple of days before I…"

He laughed again. Something inside Hannah caught fire.

"I wasn't planning on getting you pregnant tonight," he told her. "I was in the neighborhood, meeting with a potential contractor, and I thought I'd drop by and see if we could grab some dinner together.

Maybe go over our itinerary for Fiji one more time. I have a car waiting downstairs. We can go anywhere you want."

It wasn't that unusual of a request. Well, okay, the car waiting downstairs was a little outside her usual experiences, since Hannah normally bused or trained it everywhere. Even so, it took her a moment to reply.

"Anywhere?" she finally repeated. Because, if he was offering, she did have something kind of specific in mind.

"Anywhere," he promised.

"Okay," she said. "Dinner would be good. Just let me get my coat."

In retrospect, Yeager decided a couple of hours later, maybe he shouldn't have told Hannah they could go anywhere she wanted. Because she'd chosen the Russian Tea Room. Not that he had anything against it, but…it was the Russian Tea Room, which wasn't exactly his cup of tea. But Hannah had never been before and had always wanted to go, so here they were. And, truth be told, his cheese and cherry blintze had been pretty freaking amazing.

It wasn't even nine o'clock when they exited the restaurant, and Yeager didn't want the evening to end just yet. He didn't have to be at the airport for his flight to Vancouver until eleven tomorrow morning, so it wasn't like he had to be in bed early. He started to ask Hannah what else she wanted to do, but hesitated. She might tell him she wanted to go to the roof of the Empire State Building. Or, worse, on one of those cruises to see the Statue of Liberty. Or, worst of all, go ice-skating under the Christmas tree at Rockefeller Center.

He risked it anyway. "What do you want to do next?"

And heard an answer that was far, far worse.

"Can we take a carriage ride around Central Park?"

Yeager flinched as if she'd just hit him with a brick. Seriously? What was this, Prom Night?

Then he remembered how she'd once told him she hadn't gone to her prom because no one had asked her and she'd been too scared to ask anyone herself. She'd just transferred to a new school a few months before all the senior events started happening. All the kids had steered clear of her once they learned she was in the system because they'd figured she was, at best, a weirdo and, at worst, a psycho.

"Please, Yeager?" she asked, sounding very much like a high school senior who'd just moved to a new school and had no friends. "It'll be so much fun. The Christmas lights will be up in Central Park, and it's supposed to snow."

Oh, good. The only thing that would make a carriage ride through Central Park more fun would be doing it in a snow globe they could buy later from some guy in a trench coat in Times Square. But Hannah's heart was in her eyes again. Standing there in her red coat with its multicolored buttons, her striped scarf wound around her neck what looked like a dozen times, her mittened hands before her in a way that made her look like she was praying he would say yes...

He sighed with resignation. "Yeah, okay. Why not?"

Her eyes went incandescent at that and, somehow, he minded a lot less that he was doing the crass tourist thing in New York with Hannah when he could have, quite literally, been anywhere in the world doing anything he wanted. He liked being here with Hannah. He liked being anywhere with her. It didn't matter what they were doing.

They found a free carriage at 7th Avenue and 59th Street. The driver introduced himself as Yuri and his horse as Arthur, the latter delighting Hannah since, as she told Yeager, she'd never been this close to a horse before. When Yuri heard that, he handed her a carrot to feed the animal and, by her reaction as she fed Arthur, she might as well have been donning the Crown Jewels. Then they climbed into the white carriage with red velvet seats and settled in for the ride, nestled under a red-and-black-plaid blanket to chase away the chill.

Central Park opened up before them like a Christmas card, surrounding them with a winter wonderland of lamplight and moonlight and twinkling white tree lights. All was calm, all was bright, with silver lanes aglow and kids jingle-belling and chestnut vendors roasting their fare on an open fire and passersby dressed up like Eskimos. Barely ten minutes in, snow began to swirl around them, giving everything an otherworldly glow and buffering the sounds of this frosty symphony. Hannah looped her arm through his as if it were the most natural thing in the world to do, leaning her head on his shoulder. And Yeager had to admit there were worse ways to spend an evening than inside a Christmas snow globe with Hannah Robinson.

They rode in silence for a little while then Hannah sighed with much feeling. "I knew it would be like this," she said.

"Like what?" Yeager asked.

She hesitated, sighed again and whispered, "Magical."

On any other night, with any other person, Yeager would have said that was ridiculous. There was no such thing as magic. This was just Central Park, a place they both must have visited dozens of times. Lights ran on electricity. Snow was just frozen pieces of water. There was an explanation for every single thing around them.

Except, maybe, for why he wanted so badly to kiss her when there was no reason to do it.

"When you were a kid," she said quietly, "did you believe in Santa Claus?"

"Of course I believed in Santa Claus," he told her. Hell, he'd held out on the Santa-being-real thing way longer than his classmates, something that had brought him no end of ribbing. He hadn't cared. He'd been absolutely certain a white-bearded man dressed in red came down their chimney every year to scatter toys across every inch of the living room, leaving cookie crumbs and a half-empty glass of milk behind. What other explanation could there be? Such had been the innocence of his childhood. An innocence that was shattered one night in upstate New York, when his mother called him from almost a thousand miles away to tell him he would never see his father alive again.

"How about you?" he asked Hannah, pushing the memory as far to the back of his brain as he could. He thought she would reply the same way. So he wasn't quite prepared for the answer she gave him.

"I don't think I ever had the chance to believe in him. I mean, maybe when I lived with my mom before she died, I did. I don't know. But I don't remember ever looking out the window, up at the sky, waiting for his arrival. Someone must have told me at one of my first homes that there was no such thing as Santa."

When he and Hannah had their baby, Yeager thought, no one was ever going to do that. Every child should have the opportunity to believe in magic for as long as they wanted to believe. Even if Yeager didn't believe in it anymore.

"Did you at least have presents to open on Christmas morning?" he asked.

"Usually."

Usually, he echoed to himself. Meaning there had been some Christmas mornings when Hannah had gone without the breathtaking exhilaration that came with ripping brightly colored paper off boxes to see what treasure was inside. That wasn't going to happen to their child, either.

"What kind of Christmas traditions did your family have?" she asked. Probably because she'd never been in one place long enough to establish traditions of her own.

There was a time when Yeager would have refused to answer, since he generally hated talking about his parents and the life he'd had with them. That life just didn't feel like it was his anymore. In a way, it felt like it had happened to someone else. With Hannah, though, he didn't mind talking about it so much. With Hannah, that life didn't seem so alien. It didn't feel so far away.

"Every Christmas Eve," he said, "my mom made Cornish hens, with sweet potatoes and Brussels sprouts as a side."

None of which he'd eaten since her death.

"We had this Christmas china she got somewhere," he continued, "and she'd break it out for that meal and Christmas Day, then it would be boxed up again and stowed for another year."

Yeager still had that china. Somewhere. For some reason, he hadn't been able to part with it when it came to disposing of his parents' possessions after graduating from college. Maybe he'd look around for it this year. Break it out before Christmas. Maybe he and Hannah could—

But he wouldn't be in New York for Christmas, he reminded himself. He had long-standing plans to be skiing with friends in Vail.

"I got to open one gift on Christmas Eve," he continued for Hannah, "and I always took about an hour to pick out which one. Christmas morning, I wasn't allowed to get out of bed before eight, even though I was always awake by six. But at one second after eight, I'd run downstairs and behold the glory that was Christmas morning."

For the first time in a long, long time, he was able to smile at the recollections. Hell, it was surprising that he was even able to tolerate the memories in the first place. How the tree lights would be on when he awoke, even though his father was adamant they be turned off before he went to bed. How, somehow, there were already cinnamon rolls baking in the oven and hot chocolate heating on the stove and Christmas carols playing on the CD player. Back then, he'd put it all down to Santa. Santa and the magic of Christmas.

He told Hannah about all that and more, until the snow was falling furiously around them and he was dipping his head toward hers and she was lifting hers in return to meet him halfway. Their lips connected gently at first, the subtle brush of their mouths against each other a warm counterpoint to the night around them.

They chatted and canoodled for the rest of the ride around the park. When Yuri pulled Arthur to a halt where they had begun, Yeager was surprised by the depth of his disappointment. Part of him wanted to go around again. But another part of him—a bigger part—just wanted to be alone with Hannah.

As they drew up in front of her building in the car he'd hired for the day, he grew more disconcerted. Why did he feel so annoyed at having to say good-night to her? He'd be seeing her again in Fiji in a few days. For some reason, though, the days between now and then felt like an interminable—intolerable—period of time. But how to finagle an invitation to…oh, he didn't know…spend the night with her, without sounding like a jerk.

"So, Hannah, what would you think if maybe I—"

"So, Yeager, is there any chance you might want to—" she said at the same time.

They stopped talking as one, their gazes connecting. Then, as one, they both smiled.

"I think it's a great idea," she told him.

"I'd love to," he said at the same time.

He sent the driver on his way after that, empty-
ing his wallet for the tip, not wanting to waste any
more time doing something as mundane as keeping
track of his cash flow.

Hand in hand, he and Hannah climbed the stairs
to her apartment and entered. The moment they were
inside with the door closed behind them, he kissed
her. Strangely, it wasn't like the kisses that had preceded their couplings in other places. It wasn't hot
and urgent, filled with need. It was slow and sweet,
almost innocent, as if this were the first time for both
of them, and neither was sure exactly what to do.

Later, Yeager wouldn't even remember moving
the love seat to pull down the Murphy bed. Later,
he wouldn't remember the two of them undressing
each other and climbing into it. Later, he would only
remember making love to Hannah in a way they
hadn't made love before. With care and attention, and
something else that hadn't been there earlier, either.
Something he wasn't sure how to describe or what to
call. But it felt as natural and necessary as breathing.

After they spent themselves, when he wrapped
his arms around her and pulled her close, she nestled into him and tucked her head beneath his chin.
As Hannah slept beside him, Yeager looked out the
window—the only window she had onto the world—
and watched the snow fall.

And he wondered what he was going to do if he
and Hannah weren't successful with their final at-

tempt at conception in Fiji. Worse, he wondered what he was going to do after their baby was born, when he would be moving in and out of their lives, and Hannah would never have a need for a night like this again.

Nine

Hannah was throwing the last of her toiletries into the suitcase she'd be carting to Fiji in an hour when her phone rang. She wasn't surprised to see Yeager on the Caller ID, since he always called just before she was due to leave to remind her to bring sunscreen—even to Scotland—which she'd always already packed.

She thumbed the answer button and lifted the phone to her ear. "Yes, I packed sunscreen, and yes, it's SPF thirty," she greeted him.

Silence met her from the other end for a moment. Then, in a quiet, too steady voice, Yeager replied, "Hannah, I have some bad news."

Something seized up in her chest at the absolute

absence of emotion in his voice. She'd never heard him sound this way before. "Are you okay?"

"Yes," he told her quickly. "But I'm not in Vancouver."

He was supposed to have been in Vancouver yesterday afternoon, West Coast time. He'd planned to check out a site for some new mountain adventure today, then take a late-night flight that would put him in Suva before breakfast on Sunday morning, Fiji time, which would be Saturday afternoon New York time. That gave them plenty of time to get settled, since that would be the day before Hannah was set to ovulate. They'd planned everything down to the minute. At least, they had before Yeager turned up someplace he wasn't supposed to be.

"Where are you?" she asked.

He muttered an exasperated sound. "I'm in Alberta. Long story short, what was supposed to be an uneventful flight, both time- and weather-wise, got delayed a couple of hours, then a storm blew in out of nowhere just as we were approaching the Rockies. The jet I chartered had to make an emergency landing on a little airstrip at a research station in the middle of nowhere."

Hannah's tension increased with every word he spoke. "That happened yesterday?"

"Yeah."

"Why didn't you call me?"

"I didn't think it would be that big a deal. I figured the storm would blow over and we'd still make it to Vancouver today. Worst case scenario, I'd have to cancel my day trip to look at the property I'm interested in and just head right on to Fiji as planned."

"So you think you'll still be able to do that?"

His answer was way too quick for her liking. "No."

Okay, so they wouldn't be going to Fiji. That was all right. Hannah hadn't been all that keen on flying fifteen hours one way, anyway, with or without a fertility volcano—and Yeager—at the end of the journey. She was totally okay with their next attempt at conception being right here in New York. They could check into a nice hotel, have dinner—maybe even take another carriage ride around Central Park, which, of all the experiences she'd shared with Yeager, had been, hands down, the most enjoyable. Well, except for all their, um, attempts at conception.

"So I guess we're not going to Fiji then," she said.

"No," he told her. "I'm definitely not going to get out of here in time for that."

He still sounded way too somber for her liking. Way too serious. Way too worried.

"Well, when will you be able to leave?" she asked.

This time, there was a long pause followed by a quiet, "I honestly don't know."

Now Hannah felt somber, serious and worried, too. "Why not?"

"Because we're completely snowed in here. And another storm is coming right at us."

She told herself not to panic. There was still plenty of time for him to get back to New York, right? Sunday was still two days away. A flight from Alberta couldn't take more than four or five hours, could it? A third of the time it would have taken to fly to Fiji.

"But you'll be back in New York by Sunday, right?" she asked.

There was another pause, longer this time. Then a very weary-sounding Yeager told her, "I don't know, Hannah."

"But—"

"The jet took a beating before we landed. My pilot almost didn't get us to the ground in one piece."

Her nerves went barbed-wire sharp at that. "Yeager! You nearly died? And you didn't call me yesterday to tell me?"

What the hell was the matter with him? Okay, yeah, they weren't girlfriend and boyfriend, so he wasn't obligated to keep her apprised of everything that happened in his life, even when his life was threatened. But they were friends, weren't they? Kind of? Sort of? In a way? Okay, maybe they weren't friends, either—she wasn't sure what they were, actually. But they *were* trying to make a baby together, so the least he could do was keep her informed about things that put him in danger.

Then she remembered he made his living courting danger. He lived his life courting danger. Yeager wasn't happy unless he was thumbing his nose at death with some kind of crazy adventure. Nearly crashing into the side of a mountain in a private jet was probably nothing compared to some of the activities he undertook. How could she have thought it would be a good idea to have a baby with a guy like that? She was going to be worrying about the safety of her child's father for the rest of her life.

Or not. Because it was starting to sound like they might miss their last chance for her to conceive before the time ran out on the Linden fortune. If Yeager got stuck in Alberta much longer…

"The jet landed safely," he hurried to reassure her. "But not before it developed some mechanical problems that are going to keep it grounded until it can be repaired. And this place is totally closed off by road this time of year. The only way in and out is by plane, and there aren't any others here right now. Even if this new storm subsides soon, I'm going to be stuck until someone else can get in and fly us out. And I just don't know how long that will take. There must be three feet of snow on the ground."

With every word he spoke, Hannah's fears grew worse. Not just for Yeager's safety, but that the last chance she had to conceive a child with him—to start a family with him—was gone. Sunday was supposed to be her fertile day. She knew that an egg, once dropped, could be viable for, at best, twenty-four hours. If her calculations were correct—though, honestly, she had no idea these days if they were, and the fertility monitors and ovulation tests she'd tried to use hadn't been all that helpful—she could still become pregnant if Yeager made it back to New York by Monday night.

Maybe. Possibly. Perhaps.

But if he didn't make it back by then, that was it. No baby for Hannah. No Linden fortune that would have ensured the rest of her life was a happy, safe, secure one. Instead she'd be dogged forever by the specter of what might have been.

She tried not to think about the irony. Had she never discovered she was the missing Linden heir, the rest of her life would have been happy. Happy enough, anyway. She would have lived it as she always had, day by day, satisfied with what she had, working toward a future she hoped and dreamed would eventually happen. She would have had a vague idea about starting a family someday, but wouldn't have been in any big hurry. And if it never happened, well, that probably would have been okay, because she never would have known what she was missing. But now…

Now she would have to live with the very real knowledge that she wanted a family badly and might never have one. Worse, now she knew she wanted that family with Yeager, and she would never have him, either. Without him as the father of her child, there would be no reason for him to stay in her life. Not as anything other than one of her regulars at Cathcart and Quinn—though one she would now know quite a bit better than most. The only reason he would have continued to be a part of her life otherwise would have been because he was her baby's father. He wasn't the kind of man to settle down in one place with one woman—any woman. Sure, he was determined to be a father to their child, but only between trips to all four corners of the world. His idea of parenting would be swooping in with *Matryoshka* dolls and *Mozartkugel* and didgeridoos to regale his progeny with stories of his travels, then fly off again for another adventure—most likely with someone named Luydmila or Fritzi or Sheila.

Yes, Yeager Novak wanted to be a father. But he didn't want to be a *father*. Not the kind who dealt with the skinned knees and carpools and picket fences. Or with the hand-holding strolls and the Sunday-morning snuggles and the firefly-spattered evenings on the patio after the kids went to bed, the way Hannah wanted to be a mother. And the way she wanted to be—she might as well admit it—a wife.

So if Yeager didn't make it back to New York soon...

"Well, when do you think someone will be able to fly you out?" she asked.

There was another one of those uncomfortable silences. "I just don't know, Hannah. I'm sorry."

"It's okay," she told him. Even if it wasn't. Even if it kind of felt like she was stranded alone in an icy, isolated wilderness herself. "I'm sure you'll get out of there soon. I'm not supposed to ovulate until Sunday. Maybe it'll even happen Monday. As long as we can get together by Tuesday, we should be fine. You'll be back by Tuesday, right?"

The silence that met her for that reply was the worst one yet. So was the hopeless, defeated tone in Yeager's voice when he said, "Yeah. Sure. Sure, I will. It'll be fine. Look, I'm sorry, but I have to go. The power here is iffy, too, right now, and I'm not sure how long I'll have my battery. I'll call you again when I can, okay? Let you know what's going on."

"Okay," Hannah said. "Keep me posted. And, Yeager?"

"Yeah?"

She knew he hated to hear the words, but she was going to say them, anyway. "Be careful."

"I will," he said.

And that, more than anything, told her all she needed to know. He was worried, too.

She said goodbye and thumbed off the phone, then looked at the suitcase she hadn't yet closed. On top was the lacy underwear Yeager had given to her in Malta. She'd worn it every trip since, thinking it would bring them luck. And also because of the look in Yeager's eyes whenever he saw her wearing it. Automatically, she began removing everything she'd packed, piece by piece, putting it all back where it belonged. Then she gazed at the empty suitcase, feeling every bit as empty.

She told herself there was probably still time to go the sperm bank route. She'd finished the application process last summer and been cleared while she was waiting for Yeager to see a doctor about his health to ensure he was up to the task of conceiving a child. It was possible they might be able to accommodate her, especially if she explained the situation to them. She might still be able to conceive a baby this month with some anonymous donor.

But she didn't want to have a baby with some anonymous donor. She wanted Yeager to be the father of any child she might have. Having a baby wasn't about winning the Linden billions anymore. It hadn't been about that for a long time. Hannah didn't want to just start a family, not even for a family fortune. She wanted to start a family with Yeager. Because, somewhere along the line, Yeager had begun to feel like family.

Surely he'd make it home by Tuesday. Surely her egg would wait until he was there before it made an appearance. Surely this time—this last, final time— would be the one that worked.

Surely it would. Surely.

It took Yeager a full week after becoming stranded in Alberta to get back to New York, much too late for him and Hannah to even attempt conception. For the last couple of months she'd been using one of those prediction kits that indicated a surge in some hormone that happened prior to ovulation. By Wednesday afternoon, when Yeager finally called her to tell her he would be flying out the next day, that surge was nonexistent. Hannah's egg had come and gone without him. They'd never stood a chance.

He'd told her on Sunday night to go to the sperm bank on Monday and get pregnant that way. But she'd said she would wait for him. He'd been surprised by her decision—she was almost certainly not going to get pregnant if she waited for him to get back to New York, and by the time they could try next month, it would be past the legal deadline for her to inherit. But a part of him had been delighted by her decision, too. He still liked the idea of having a child with Hannah. Now, though, there wouldn't be any financial benefit to her, so he couldn't see her wanting to continue the effort.

Even if he offered to pay for everything the child needed—and then some—he couldn't see her going along. Hannah wanted to make her own way in the world. She wanted to have a child on her terms, not his, which was perfectly understandable. But she wouldn't be able to do that until she was at a place in her life where having a child fit in. Now that she wouldn't be claiming her family fortune, who knew when she'd be able to swing it? And by the time she could, there would probably be some other guy in the picture who could provide the paternity. And maybe provide a life with her, too. She wouldn't need Yeager for any of it. Not that he wanted to spend a life with Hannah—or any woman. But the idea of her starting a family with someone else now was just… inconceivable. No pun intended.

He wished her grandfather was still alive. Not just so Yeager could tell the guy what an incredible granddaughter he had—so it was unfair to put some ridiculous condition on her inheritance like insisting she have a child—but also so he could strangle the guy with his bare hands. Seriously, what kind of jerk turned a woman into an incubator, just so he could ensure his family line remained intact?

Okay, so, in a way, maybe Yeager had kind of done that to Hannah, too. That was beside the point. The point was…

He sighed with much feeling as he gazed out the window of his office at the snow falling over New York. The point was that he and Hannah had both wanted a child for their own reasons, and now they wouldn't be having one. What could either of them say or do at this point that would make that better? It wasn't like either of them was at fault for what had happened, but that didn't make it any easier to bear.

So where did that leave them? What would they be to each other now? It wasn't like they could go back to just being seamstress and client. But they didn't

feel like just friends, either. Sure, they were lovers—
or maybe former lovers—but even that didn't feel
like the right word to use. Yeager had had lots of
lovers—and he had lots of former lovers—but he'd
never felt for any of them the way he felt for Hannah.

He forced himself to turn away from the window
and go back to his desk, where a mountain of work
awaited him after his stay in Alberta. He told himself he was way overthinking this. He and Hannah
were friends. Period. That was why he felt differ-
ently about her than he had other women he'd dated.
Those women had been great, and he'd liked all of
them, but they'd never been…Hannah. And he didn't
kid himself that he'd ever meet another woman who
was like her. Who would be a *friend* like her, he corrected himself. Women would come and go in his
life the way they always had, but Hannah would be
constant. The way friends were.

Yeah, that was it. They were friends. Friends who
would stay friends, no matter what. Even if they
didn't have a child to tie them together. Wouldn't
they?

Surely they would. Surely.

Hannah awoke on New Year's Day with *the*
weirdest feeling, after having some of *the* weirdest
dreams she'd ever had. In one, she was underwater,
but perfectly capable of breathing, and was suddenly
surrounded by and swimming among dolphins. In

another, she was tending to a garden full of lotuses and turtles kept coming up out of the soil. Yeager was in another, bringing her a basket of acorns that she upended and consumed in one gulp. Just…weird.

She also realized she'd slept way past the usual time she awoke on days when Cathcart and Quinn was closed. It was nearly eleven when she finally opened her eyes and looked at the clock.

Still feeling as if someone had wrapped her in cotton gauze, she rolled over and, for some reason, settled both hands over her lower abdomen, splaying her fingers wide. It shouldn't have been an unusual gesture. Except that she never did it. Usually, when she awoke and turned to lie on her back in bed, she tucked both hands behind her head. What the hell was up with those dreams, and why did she have her hands on her abdomen instead of—

Heat suddenly flared in her belly. She dared not hope…but did anyway. Was her body trying to tell her brain something it hadn't yet figured out? Like maybe…

She was supposed to have started her period yesterday or the day before, but she'd put down the lateness as a result of, number one, her cycle never being all that regular to begin with and, two, the stress of the last several months taking its toll. She shouldn't have been fertile the night she and Yeager made love in New York, and sperm normally weren't viable for more than three days after they launched. On the other hand, she'd read that it was possible for some of those little swimmers to hang around for five days after their release. And, hey, it *was* Yeager's little swimmers she was talking about.

It was also possible she'd dropped an egg before she thought she would. Those ovulation predictor kits were iffy. They only told you your hormones were in the right place for you to ovulate, but not exactly when you would. So maybe, *maybe*, that snowy night when they'd made love right here in her bed, the circumstances had been right.

She had a pregnancy kit in her bathroom she'd bought after their last attempt failed. Her hands were actually shaking as she withdrew it from the medicine cabinet. And she didn't think she took a single breath while she counted down the seconds it took for the indicator to produce the word *Yes* or *No*. Five times she had performed this ritual. Five times, it had ended with the word *No*. She waited a full minute longer than she needed to to check the results this morning. And she had one eye closed, and the other narrowed, when she finally picked up the indicator to look at it. So it was no wonder she was still doubtful when she saw that the answer this time was—

Yes.

Heat exploded inside her at those three little letters. She didn't believe it. Couldn't believe it. Wouldn't believe it until she took a second test. Which she didn't have. So she yanked on some pants and threw her coat on over her pajama shirt, tugged snow boots on over her bare feet, grabbed her wallet and ran downstairs to the *mercado* below her apartment…only to find it closed for the holiday.

She knew a moment of panic. Until she remembered the twenty-four-hour Duane Reade two blocks up. She knew it was closed on Thanksgiving and Christmas. Oh, *pleasepleaseplease*, Pregnancy Gods and Goddesses, don't let it be closed on New Year's, too.

The gods and goddesses were good to Hannah that day because a half hour later she was counting down to see the results of the second test. The sample wouldn't be nearly as strong as the first, because she'd been storing up that one all night, and this one was the result of two hastily consumed cups of coffee purchased along with the pregnancy test. But even with the weakened sample, when she picked up the wand, studying it with both eyes wide open this time, the word she saw was—

Yes.

No matter how many times Hannah looked at it, and no matter from what angle, the word she saw, again and again, was *Yes.*

Yes. *Yes.* YES. *Yessssss!*

Holy cow. She was going to have a baby. She and Yeager were going to have a baby. She was going to have a family. A real family. The way she'd always wanted. The way she'd never really thought she would.

She had to tell him. Immediately. In person. She could shower and change and be at his place by—

By never, because she realized in that moment that she didn't even know where he lived. There had never been a reason to visit him at his place, and other than one vague mention of his having a condo in West Chelsea, the topic of where he lived had never come up in their conversations. Why should it? There had never been a reason for her to visit him at home, and there never would be, unless—until— they had a child together. Which had seemed less and less likely with every passing month.

They weren't boyfriend and girlfriend, she reminded herself for perhaps the hundredth time since going into this venture with him. They weren't even lovers, at least not on Yeager's part. It didn't matter that Hannah was battling some weird emotions on that front herself. Maybe she had grown to love him over the last six months—maybe—but she would fall out of love again, once the two of them weren't so involved. Right? Of course.

They were partners. That was all. And they would always be partners, thanks to this baby. But it was more like a business arrangement than anything else. They'd even signed paperwork outlining their obligations to each other during the conception process and to the child once its conception was achieved. They had each gone into it with individual needs and goals, and this baby—they were going to have a baby!—would fulfill those needs and goals for each of them. Yes, that sounded kind of indifferent and calculating, but that was exactly what their agreement had been at first. Nothing personal. Everything planned. And now...

A wave of something that was in no way indifferent or calculating—or impersonal or unplanned—rolled through her midsection. Oh, God. Now it was so, *so* much more than any of those things. Now it was...it was...

She grabbed her phone to text Yeager, asking him only where he was. They hadn't spoken since his return to New York—probably because neither of them had known what to say. He might not even be in New York at the moment. How did billionaire adventurers celebrate New Year's Eve, anyway? For all she knew, he'd followed the holiday around the world, celebrating it a dozen times, starting in Samoa and ending in Pago Pago.

He texted back immediately, telling her he was at home. Why?

She didn't want to announce something like this with a text. Or even a phone call. So her text back to him was simple, if vague. Would it be okay if I came over for a little while?

He again replied immediately. Sure. Everything ok?

Fine, she returned. Just want to talk. Then she

backspaced over the last part before hitting Send and amended it to Just need to talk.

Yeager texted back his address on West 21st and said he'd be working at home all day. Hannah told him she'd be there in an hour or so. The 7 train on holidays never ran very efficiently, after all. Fortunately for Hannah, though, her body finally was.

Ten

Damn the 7 train, anyway, Yeager thought as he waited for Hannah's arrival nearly two hours later. It never ran well on holidays.

He'd given up trying to work after she'd sent her last text, because he'd been too busy wondering what she needed to talk about. He'd at least showered and shaved and changed into a pair of jeans and an oatmeal-colored sweater, but that had only eaten up about thirty minutes. For the last—he glanced at the Bavarian clock on his mantel nestled between the Turkish *Iznik* bowl and a Puerto Rican *vejigante* mask—seventy-eight minutes, he'd done little more than pace from room to room trying to find something to occupy himself. He hadn't even eaten lunch because his stomach was too full of apprehension.

Two hours and sixteen minutes after Hannah's last text, there was finally a knock at his front door—Yeager had already notified Baxter, the doorman, that he was expecting her and to send her right up. He couldn't believe how nervous he was when he went to answer the door. As he strode down the long gallery from the living room where he'd been pacing, it did that cinematic stretch thing where it seemed to quadruple in length.

It had just been too long since he'd seen her, that was all. Since July, they'd never gone more than a couple of weeks without contact. Then he realized it had only been a couple of weeks since he and Hannah had taken that carriage ride through Central Park. No different from most other months and hardly an eon. Even if it did feel like one.

He opened his front door to find her standing there in her red coat with the funny, different-colored buttons that she'd designed and made herself, her striped scarf tripled around her neck. Her hair was damp and glistening from the snow that had begun to fall not long after she'd texted. And her eyes…

Damn. Those eyes. Even after knowing her as long as he had, even after making love to her a dozen times, her eyes still seized something deep inside him and held fast. Yeager would always be startled by the clarity and depth of emotion in Hannah's eyes.

"Hi," she said.

Still feeling as nervous as a schoolboy at his first dance—even though he hadn't even been this nervous as a schoolboy at his first dance—he replied, "Hi."

He took a step backward and gestured her inside, and she strode past him slowly, almost cautiously, as if she weren't sure of her reception here. Why was this the first time she'd ever been in his home? He should have invited her over a long time ago.

He closed the door behind her and followed her down the gallery, Hannah unwinding her scarf as she went. By the time they reached his living room with its panoramic windows on both sides, she had shrugged it off, along with her coat. Beneath, she was wearing jeans and a fuzzy white sweater. She transferred her coat restlessly from one hand to the other.

"Let me take your coat," Yeager said, reaching toward it.

She looked a little confused by the gesture at first, as if her thoughts were a million miles away. Then she awkwardly extended her coat to him. He awkwardly took it from her. Then he shifted it from one hand to the other a couple of times before tossing it onto the chair nearest him.

"So," he began…then realized he had no idea what else to say. Finally he went with, "How've you been?"

And immediately regretted the question. How the

hell did he think she'd been? She wasn't going to
have the family or the fortune that had been dangled
in front of her for six months then cruelly yanked
away from her to leave her with neither. He was
going to go out on a limb and say she hadn't been
too great.

Instead of replying, she darted her gaze around
his living room, from the travel trophies on his man-
telpiece to the Russian mosaic on the wall above
them to the Chilean pottery lining one windowsill
to the Indonesian shadow puppets hanging above
the door to his office. Her gaze seemed to light on
every item he'd ever brought home with him from
his adventures—and there were scores of them in
this room alone.

Finally she looked at him again. "I didn't think
you'd be home," she said softly.

"Why not?"

"I just figured you'd be somewhere else. I mean,
look at this place, Yeager. It's incredible. How many
people can live the way you do? I just thought you'd
be celebrating New Year's somewhere besides New
York, that's all."

He started to tell her he hadn't felt like celebrating. The New Year or anything else. Instead he told
her, "I have a lot that needs attention here right now."

One of those things should have been Hannah.
One of those things was Hannah. He just wasn't

sure yet what kind of attention to direct her way. He wasn't sure he'd ever know.

"Hannah, is everything okay?" he asked.

She opened her mouth to reply then something over his shoulder caught her eye. She moved to the side of his living room that looked out onto the Hudson.

"You can see the Statue of Liberty from here," she said.

Yeager had forgotten about that. He'd lived here long enough that he guessed he took it for granted. And why the hell wasn't she answering his question?

She walked to the other side of the living room and looked out the windows there. "And you can see the Empire State Building from here," she said.

Yeah, he'd forgotten about that, too. He'd honestly stopped seeing the views as anything other than New York City in general and Manhattan in particular. Not that he didn't appreciate the view, he just hadn't really given it much thought in the last few years. To someone like Hannah, though, who'd spent who knew how long in her cramped Sunnyside studio with one window that looked at the apartment building on the next street, his view of the city was doubtless pretty incredible.

Why had he forgotten about that when it was what had impressed him about the place so much the first time he'd looked at it? The minute he'd seen the views Hannah had just seen, the little boy from

Peoria had surged up inside him and hadn't been able to believe it was possible to see so much from one room. It was like looking at the whole, wide world in one swoop. And at night, when the city lights were on, it was like the world went on *forever*.

When Hannah turned to look at him again, she had tears in her eyes. The only other times Yeager had seen her cry were the night he'd initially turned down her request that he be the father of her child and that first time she'd come to his office to tell him she wasn't pregnant. Both times she'd been in a position where she thought she would miss out on inheriting her family's fortune—or, at least, that was why he'd thought she was crying at the time. He knew now that the money wasn't the primary reason Hannah had wanted to get pregnant—she genuinely wanted to start the family she'd never thought she might have. But, come on—who wouldn't cry at the prospect of losing billions of dollars? Yeager almost felt like crying himself.

Even so, it had been weeks since they'd realized they wouldn't make the deadline for the terms of her grandfather's will. Why was she crying now?

"Hannah?" He tried again. "Are you okay?"

She nodded, wiping at each eye. "Yeah, I am. It's just that standing here, looking at your place… It's just… It's *huge*, Yeager. And it's gorgeous. It embodies everything good that money can make happen. All morning, I've only been thinking about what it will be like to finally have a family. I'm just now re-membering I'll have enough money to live the way you do. I'd actually forgotten about that. Isn't that weird? When I realized this morning that I'm preg-nant, I didn't even think about the Linden fortune. All I could think about was the baby and you."

Yeager had pretty much stopped hearing what she said after the words *I'm pregnant*. Probably because the roar of adrenaline that started rushing through him made it impossible to register anything else.

"You're pregnant?" he asked, his breath shallow.

She nodded.

"You're sure?"

She nodded again. "I took two tests. They were both positive. I mean, I need to see the doctor for a blood test, too, I guess, but those home tests are pretty freaking accurate."

Yeager still couldn't believe it. "But how? I was in Alberta."

Hannah laughed. "It didn't happen when you were in Alberta, obviously. It happened here in New York. That night we went to the Russian Tea Room and took the carriage ride through Central Park."

He shook his head. "So all those times we planned down to the minute, all those adventures, all those exotic places…"

She shrugged. "Turns out I just needed some spontaneity in familiar surroundings to be at my most, um, fertile."

Hey, whatever worked. That night at the Russian Tea Room and riding around Central Park with Hannah had still been an adventure, Yeager realized. He'd done things that night he'd never done before, and he'd felt as exhilarated by them as he had by any other risk he'd ever taken. Hell, any time he spent with Hannah was an adventure. They'd still be doing his legacy—and Tommy—proud.

"We're going to have a baby?" Yeager asked. Because he *still* couldn't believe he'd heard her correctly.

"Yeah, Yeager. We're going to have a baby."

They were going to have a baby. Even though they'd been working toward the goal for months, he had no idea what to say or how to act. He'd been so certain the first time they'd tried that it would happen immediately. He and Hannah could pat each other on the back and say, *Job well done.* Then they'd see each other again in a year or so—after she'd had a few months to get used to the whole motherhood thing—to arrange a visitation schedule. When he'd initially envisioned the arrangement, he hadn't seen much point in visiting the baby when he or she was still an infant, since babies couldn't communicate or interact or do much of anything but lie there and stare at you. They sure as hell couldn't travel or have adventures. But by the time the child was three or four, it would be a good time to get to know his progeny and gradually start introducing him or her to the world. Now, however...

He'd been such an idiot.

Because now, after months of disappointment and fear that he would never become a father, Yeager realized he wanted a lot more than to just put a miniature version of himself on the planet to be his legacy after he was gone. He couldn't just settle for visiting his child a couple of times a year and taking him or her on age-appropriate adventures. Sending an exotic gift and having a Skype conversation from the other side of the world on birthdays and holidays wouldn't be enough. Yeager wanted...

He wanted to be a father.

"So, pretty cool, huh?" Hannah said, her voice sounding like it was coming through an echo chamber on the other side of the planet.

Cool? Yeah, it was cool. Among other things. A million, billion other things that Yeager would be able to identify if his brain wasn't trying to light on every single one of them at the same time.

When he still didn't say anything—because he honestly couldn't figure out yet what to say—Hannah continued, less enthusiastically. "I mean, it's what we both wanted, right?"

Yeager nodded. But he still couldn't find his voice.

"I'll get my family and my family fortune," she said, "and you'll get your legacy to carry on after you're gone."

He still couldn't believe it was that easy. Then again, he knew it hadn't been easy. On either of them. But it had probably been tougher on Hannah than on him. With or without a child, his life—or, at least, his lifestyle—wasn't going to change all that much. But hers…

Now she could live her life any way she wanted to. She would have everything she'd ever hoped for, everything she'd ever wanted. A family. Financial freedom. A business empire she built all by herself. Yeager knew how gratifying all of those things could be. He was happy for Hannah. He was. It just felt kind of weird that she'd have all those things without him.

She was still looking at him expectantly, her eyes full of joy and wonder and relief, but also apprehension and fear and a host of other emotions that cut right to his soul. And then he felt the joy and wonder, too, and he realized it didn't matter that he couldn't find the words. He didn't need words. He crossed the room to where she was standing and swept her into his arms.

"We're going to have a baby," he said in the same astonished, ecstatic way she had.

And then they were laughing and staring at each other in disbelief and both of them were groping for words.

"Wow, we're really…"

"And we're…"

"I know, right? It's just so…"

"Exactly. How can…?"

"I don't know. It's just so…"

"Yeah. It really is the most…"

"And it's…"

"Totally unbelievably…"

"Awesome," they finally said as one.

And that word, more than any other Yeager knew, captured everything that needed to be said. At least for now. The rest…

Well, he'd worry about the rest of it later. Once he had it all figured out. In a million years or so.

It was dark by the time it occurred to Hannah that she should be going home. She and Yeager had spent hours trying to get accustomed to the new life growing inside her and how it was going to change *everything*. They fixed lunch together in his kitchen and ate it in his dining room, and talked some more about how the baby was going to change *everything*. Not so much for Yeager, since he would still be living his life the way he always had, arranging his schedule here and there to visit his son or daughter, but for Hannah.

She had called Gus Fiver at his home—as he'd told her to do, should there be any developments like this outside regular office hours—to tell the attorney the good news and had arranged to meet with him in a few days, after she'd had a chance to see her doctor to confirm what she already knew. She wasn't sure what kind of legal hurdles still lay ahead or what kind of time frame she was looking at for coming into her inheritance, but she figured it was probably safe at this point to give her two weeks' notice to Cathcart and Quinn. And then…

She had no idea. She had to find a bigger place to live, obviously, someplace with a yard that was close to good schools and lots of child-friendly places and activities. But she didn't want to move too far from where she lived now, since Queens was familiar and she liked it a lot. Maybe she could find a house with a nice yard in Astoria or Jackson Heights. Someplace that had a lot of families and things for families to do and places for families to go. Because once she had this baby, she would be part of a family. A family who could go anywhere and do anything and live any way they wanted.

Before the realization of that started making her woozy again, she told Yeager, "I should probably head home."

They were sitting on his sofa, gazing out the windows that faced the Empire State Building, the city sparkling like fairy lights against the black sky. When night had first fallen, Hannah thought the view breathtaking. Now, though, she marveled at how Yeager could see so much of New York from his place, but knew nothing about the people who were living out there. Maybe her tiny apartment didn't boast a spectacular view like this one, but she knew most of the people who populated it. That, she hoped, would never change, no matter where the future took her.

"Go?" Yeager echoed from beside her. He had his arm comfortably draped across the sofa behind her, his feet propped on the antique steamer trunk he used for a coffee table. His posture suggested this was something the two them did all the time instead of this being Hannah's first visit to his home. "But you just got here."

"We've been talking for hours," she said. "And it's getting late."

"Stay here tonight," he told her.

His tone of voice was as comfortable as the rest of him, but Hannah was surprised by the invitation. And she had mixed feelings about accepting it. On one hand, she absolutely wanted to spend the night with Yeager. She wanted to spend every night with him. She wanted to spend her life with him. On the other hand, their "business" together really was concluded, at least until after the baby was born. There was no reason for her to prolong her time with him. Especially since she knew that the more time she spent with him, the more difficult that parting was going to be.

"I can't," she said reluctantly. "I have to work tomorrow and I don't have any of my stuff with me."

"You can use my stuff."

The intimacy inherent in that statement made her toes curl. He was speaking as if the two of them shared this space all the time. He was probably accustomed to having his girlfriends spend the night on a regular basis—even though, Hannah reminded herself again, she wasn't his girlfriend. They weren't intimate, even if they had made love several times and were now expecting a baby. Intimacy was more than the sharing of bodies. It was the sharing of souls. It was the sharing of everything. And *everything* was the last thing Yeager wanted to share with anyone.

"I can't use your stuff," she told him. "Your clothes won't fit me."

He grinned lasciviously. "Who said anything about wearing clothes?"

Her heart raced. He still wanted to have sex with her, even without the goal of getting her pregnant. Maybe...

Maybe nothing, she told herself firmly. He was Yeager Novak. He wanted to have sex with every woman in North America. And South America. And Europe, Asia, Africa, Australia and Antarctica.

"I have to work tomorrow," she told him, hoping she only imagined the husky, sex-starved quality her voice seemed to suddenly have. "And Cathcart and Quinn has a strict dress code."

"Then don't go to work," he said.

"I have to go to work."

"Why? You're rich."

She started to tell him—again—that she wasn't rich yet, then remembered that, at this point, that was no longer true. It was merely a formality. She would be rich—her stomach pitched at the reminder. But she wouldn't breathe easy about that until everything was official. And she couldn't just quit her job impulsively. Maybe Misters Cathcart and Quinn hadn't been the most accommodating employers all the time, but they'd done her a solid favor ten years ago, giving her a job while she was still in high school with little work experience. And once she'd explained her situation with her grandfather's will, they'd granted her all the time off she needed. It would be ungrateful and mean to just walk away without warning.

"I have to give my two weeks' notice," she said. "I can't leave Cathcart and Quinn hanging without a seamstress. That would be irresponsible. Not to mention just a crappy thing to do."

She hesitated a moment, then made herself say the rest of what she had to say. Especially since she and Yeager both seemed to need to hear it spelled out. "Besides, you and I aren't… We won't be… It's not necessary for us to…" She sighed in frustration and tried again. "We don't…need each other anymore, Yeager."

Which, she told herself, was the truth. Although she needed him—although she loved him—he didn't need or love her. So the *each other* part of that statement kept it from being a lie.

His gaze locked with hers but he said nothing. Unable to tolerate the intensity of his blue, blue eyes, Hannah looked out at the city and said the rest. "I appreciate everything you've done. Oh, God, that was a terrible platitude." She hurried on when she realized what she was saying. "I just mean..." She muttered a ripe oath under her breath. "I'm honestly not sure what I can say that *won't* sound like a platitude, but I'll give it a shot."

She made herself look at him again. And wished she hadn't. Because there was something in his eyes she'd never seen before, something she couldn't identify, except to say that it wasn't good. In spite of that, she pressed on.

"Thank you for everything you've done for me over the last six months, Yeager. Not just in providing the biological essentials I needed to make a baby, but in showing me the world, too. I'm a different person, a better person now than I was five months ago, thanks to you. And not just because of the new life growing inside me. But because of other things inside me now, too."

Probably best not to dwell on those *other things*, since they included being in love for the first time in her life and the knowledge that she would never love anyone like this again.

"I know this...this venture...was time-consuming

for you and I know it kept you tethered in one place for a lot longer than you're used to being confined. I understand you need to get back to business as usual. I need to get back to business as usual, too. Even if things are going to be a lot different for me now. So you don't have to invite me to spend the night because it's getting late. I'll be okay on my own. I promise. I've been okay on my own for a long time."

She deliberately used singular pronouns when she spoke, because she knew she and Yeager weren't a collective anymore. This baby was her baby, and it was his baby, but it wasn't *their* baby. In the agreement they'd signed, Hannah alone would be responsible for her pregnancy, without any obligation on Yeager's part. She would contact him after her baby was born to see when he wanted to start visiting his son or daughter and work from there.

That was how they'd both wanted it five-and-a-half months ago. It was doubtless how Yeager still wanted it. Just because Hannah had begun to wish he would be there for her now…that he would be there for her forever… It was irrelevant. *Their* time was at an end. From here on out, Hannah would have her time, and Yeager would have his time, and they would only interact whenever he could fit a visit to his child into his schedule.

"So…thanks," she said again. "But I've got this."

Yeager studied her in silence for a long time. Then he said, "And what if I want it, too?"

Heat suffused her, but not for the same reason it usually did when Yeager looked at her the way he sometimes did. This look was certainly heated. But it was heated in a way she'd never seen before.

"What do you mean?" she asked.

He hesitated again then he said, "I mean, what if I want to be a part of your pregnancy? What if I want to be there when our baby is born?"

"I…" she began.

Then she halted. She really did want to get on with her life without Yeager as quickly and cleanly as possible. It was going to become more and more difficult to do that the longer he stayed a part of it. But her baby was his baby, too. If he wanted to be there for its birth, could she really deny him that?

"All right," she said reluctantly. "If you don't mind sticking close to New York when the due date approaches, then I'll call you when I leave for the hospital and you can be there when the baby is born."

"I can definitely stay close to New York," he said. And there was something in his voice when he said it that made it seem like he was talking about more than just for the baby's due date. "And what if I want to be… What do you call it? Like a pregnancy coach or something? What if I want to be there for your pregnancy, too?"

"I don't think there's such a thing as a pregnancy coach." Hannah hedged, avoiding an answer.

"But the person who coaches you through labor is a doula."

"Okay, so what if I want to be a doula?" he asked.

His request surprised her. "I don't know if a man can be a doula."

"It's the twenty-first century, Hannah. Gender roles are fluid."

Still stalling, she replied, "Oh, sure. Tell that to all the women making seventy-nine cents for every man's dollar."

He smiled at that. She felt a little better. Though she still felt plenty weird. Just what was Yeager asking, really?

"Then maybe I can be a dude-la," he said. "Be there for you during your pregnancy, whenever you need me. What would you think about that?"

She narrowed her eyes at him. "I think it would be tough for you to do that from places like Kyrgyzstan and Djibouti."

He lifted a shoulder and let it drop. "Like I said, I can stay close to New York."

Well, this was certainly news to Hannah. She could count on all her fingers and toes and then some the times he'd told her he could never stay in one place for too long. "Since when?" she asked.

This time Yeager didn't hesitate at all when he replied. "Since the minute you told me you're pregnant."

"You've always said you'd suffocate if you had

to stay in one place for any length of time," she reminded him.

"That's what I used to think," he agreed. "Back when I was an idiot. But now…"

"Now what?"

He sat forward, removing his feet from the steamer trunk to place them firmly on the floor. As if he were trying to anchor himself here.

"Look, I won't lie," he said. "There's still a lot I need to figure out about this whole fatherhood thing. But that's just the point, Hannah. I want to figure it out. I don't just want a legacy. I'm beginning to wonder if that was what I really wanted in the first place. I don't know. I don't know a lot of things. But there's one thing I *do* know. I want more than to be a long-distance parent."

He turned to face her fully, then lifted a hand to cup her cheek. "And I know one other thing, too," he said softly. "I want *us* to be more than long-distance parents. I want us to be more than parents, period. I don't want us to be you and me. I want us to be…us."

Hannah covered his hand with hers, worried he might take it back. Worried he might take it all back. But she had no idea what to say.

Yeager didn't seem to be finished, though, because he continued. "I've spent my adult life circling the globe, trying to find the thing that will make my pulse pound hardest, my heart hammer fastest and my soul sing loudest. I've done things no normal human being has ever done, and I've had one adrenaline buzz after another. But today, when you told me you're pregnant… Hannah, I've never felt anything like that in my life. And I'm still reeling from it. It's intoxicating, this feeling of…of…"

"Joy," she finished for him. Because she'd had more time than he to identify it for what it was.

"Yeah," he agreed. "Joy. And, yes, it's partly because of the baby, but even more, it's because of you. Even before this baby happened, I knew I wanted more with you. Since I started spending time with you, Hannah, *everything* in my life has been different. No matter where I've been, as long as I've been with you, I've been…happy. Since my parents died, I was beginning to think I'd never feel that way again. Maybe that's why I keep circling the globe—I'm looking for that. But I don't need to keep running all over the world. I only need to be where you are. Where you and our baby are. Because starting a family with the woman I love? That's the ultimate adventure. One I want to live over and over again."

Now Hannah was the one experiencing the heart-hammering, pulse-pounding, soul-singing adrenaline rush. And all because of three little words. Very softly, she asked, "You love me?"

Yeager nodded. "It may have taken me a while to figure that out, too, but I finally did. I do love you. I've probably loved you since that first trip we took together. And I will love you for the rest of my days, no matter where I spend them."

"Just for the sake of clarification," she said, not sure why she was belaboring this, "you love me for more than being able to stitch up your clothes and clean out the walrus stains, right?"

He smiled. "Yeah. For more than that. A lot more."

He waited for Hannah's response and, when it didn't come—mostly because she was too stunned to say anything—he sobered some. And he said, "Please tell me this isn't a one-sided thing. I mean, I know you were doing your best to keep us separated with all the 'I' and 'you' talk a minute ago, but I can't help feeling maybe you at least like me more than you did when we first went into this thing."

"No, I don't like you more," she told him. "I love you. Always."

His smile turned dazzling. "So what do you say then? You want to hitch our stars together? See where it takes us?"

She thought about that for a moment. And after another moment, she smiled back. "I'll agree on two conditions," she told him.

"Conditions?" he asked, smiling at the echo of their conversation six months ago.

She smiled back, obviously remembering. "Number one, we *have* to have a home base here in New York where we can put down roots. A place where we can take hand-holding strolls and have Sunday-morning snuggles and enjoy firefly-spattered evenings on the patio after the kids go to bed."

"Kids," he repeated. "As in plural?"

She nodded. "That's the second condition. We *have* to keep traveling and having adventures in exotic places to get pregnant again. I want to have lots of kids, Yeager, which means we have to have lots of epic sex."

He eyed her speculatively. "Well, okay. If we *have* to."

They smiled as one and wove their hands together. Then they leaned back on the sofa and gazed at the lights of Manhattan, marveling at what their lives ahead held. Maybe Hannah could spend the night here tonight. And maybe she could call out from work tomorrow. It would only be one day. And, hey, she and Yeager were celebrating.

"Happy New Year, Yeager," she said softly.

"Happy New Life, Hannah," he replied.

And she knew in that moment, it would be. Because no matter where life took them, no matter what adventures awaited, they were a family. And they always would be.

* * * * *

COMING NEXT MONTH FROM

HARLEQUIN®

Desire

Available January 2, 2018

#2563 THE RANCHER'S BABY
Texas Cattleman's Club: The Impostor • by Maisey Yates
When Selena Jacobs's ex-husband shows up at his own funeral, it's her estranged best friend who insists on staying with her to keep her safe. But living with the one who got away gets complicated when one night leads to an unexpected surprise...

#2564 TAMING THE TEXAN
Billionaires and Babies • by Jules Bennett
Former military man turned cowboy Hayes Elliott is back at the family ranch to recover from his injuries. The last thing he needs is to fall into bed with temptation...especially when she's a sexy single mom who used to be married to his best friend!

#2565 LITTLE SECRETS: UNEXPECTEDLY PREGNANT
by Joss Wood
Three years ago, Sage pushed Tyce away. Three months ago, they shared one (mistaken) red-hot night of passion. Now? She's pregnant and can't stay away from the man who drives her wild. But as passion turns to love, secrets and fears could threaten everything...

#2566 CLAIMING HIS SECRET HEIR
The McNeill Magnates • by Joanne Rock
Damon McNeill's wife has returned a year after leaving him—but between her amnesia and the baby boy she's cradling, he's suddenly unsure of what really happened. Will he untangle the deception and lies surrounding her disappearance in time to salvage their marriage?

#2567 CONTRACT BRIDE
In Name Only • by Kat Cantrell
CEO Warren Garinger knows better than to act on his fantasies about his gorgeous employee Tilda Barrett, but when she needs a green card marriage, he volunteers to say, "I do." Once he's her husband, though, keeping his distance is no longer an option!

#2568 PREGNANT BY THE CEO
The Jameson Heirs • by HelenKay Dimon
Derrick Jameson dedicated his life to the family business, and all he needs to close the deal is the perfect fiancée. When the sister of his nemesis shows up, desperate to make amends, it's perfect...until a surprise pregnancy brings everyone's secrets to light!

YOU CAN FIND MORE INFORMATION ON UPCOMING HARLEQUIN® TITLES, FREE EXCERPTS AND MORE AT WWW.HARLEQUIN.COM.

HDCNM1217

Get 2 Free Books,

Plus 2 Free Gifts—

just for trying the Reader Service!

YES! Please send me 2 FREE Harlequin® Desire novels and my 2 FREE gifts (gifts are worth about $10 retail). After receiving them, if I don't wish to receive any more books, I can return the shipping statement marked "cancel." If I don't cancel, I will receive 6 brand-new novels every month and be billed just $4.55 per book in the U.S. or $5.24 per book in Canada. That's a savings of at least 13% off the cover price! It's quite a bargain! Shipping and handling is just 50¢ per book in the U.S. and 75¢ per book in Canada.* I understand that accepting the 2 free books and gifts places me under no obligation to buy anything. I can always return a shipment and cancel at any time. The free books and gifts are mine to keep no matter what I decide.

225/326 HDN GMRV

Name	(PLEASE PRINT)

Address   Apt. #

City   State/Prov.   Zip/Postal Code

Signature (if under 18, a parent or guardian must sign)

Mail to the **Reader Service:**
IN U.S.A.: P.O. Box 1341, Buffalo, NY 14240-8531
IN CANADA: P.O. Box 603, Fort Erie, Ontario L2A 5X3

Want to try two free books from another line?
Call 1-800-873-8635 or visit www.ReaderService.com.

*Terms and prices subject to change without notice. Prices do not include applicable taxes. Sales tax applicable in N.Y. Canadian residents will be charged applicable taxes. Offer not valid in Quebec. This offer is limited to one order per household. Books received may not be as shown. Not valid for current subscribers to Harlequin Desire books. All orders subject to approval. Credit or debit balances in a customer's account(s) may be offset by any other outstanding balance owed by or to the customer. Please allow 4 to 6 weeks for delivery. Offer available while quantities last.

Your Privacy—The Reader Service is committed to protecting your privacy. Our Privacy Policy is available online at www.ReaderService.com or upon request from the Reader Service.

We make a portion of our mailing list available to reputable third parties that offer products we believe may interest you. If you prefer that we not exchange your name with third parties, or if you wish to clarify or modify your communication preferences, please visit us at www.ReaderService.com/consumerschoice or write to us at Reader Service Preference Service, P.O. Box 9062, Buffalo, NY 14240-9062. Include your complete name and address.

HDI7R2

*When Selena Jacobs's ex-husband shows up at his own
funeral, it's her estranged best friend who insists on
staying with her to keep her safe. But living with
The One Who Got Away gets complicated when one night
leads to an unexpected surprise...*

*Read on for a sneak peek at
THE RANCHER'S BABY
by New York Times bestselling author Maisey Yates,
the first book in the
TEXAS CATTLEMAN'S CLUB: THE IMPOSTOR series!*

She wandered out of the kitchen and into the living room just
as the door to the guest bedroom opened and Knox walked out,
pulling his T-shirt over his head—but not quickly enough. She
caught a flash of muscled, tanned skin and...

She was completely immobilized by the sight of her best
friend's muscles.

It wasn't like she had never seen Knox shirtless before.
But it had been a long time. And the last time, he had most
definitely been married.

Not that she had forgotten he was hot when he was married
to Cassandra. It was just that...he had been a married man. And
that meant something to Selena. Because it meant something
to him.

It had been a barrier, an insurmountable one, even bigger
than that whole long-term friendship thing. And now it wasn't
there. It just wasn't. He was walking out of the guest bedroom
looking sleep rumpled and entirely too lickable. And there was

just…nothing stopping them from doing what men and women did.

She'd had a million excuses for not doing that. For a long time. She didn't want to risk entanglements, didn't want to compromise her focus. Didn't want to risk pregnancy. Didn't have time for a relationship.

But she was in a place where those things were less of a concern. This house was symbolic of that change in her life. She was making a home. And making a home made her want to fill it. With art, with warmth, with knickknacks that spoke to her.

With people.

She wondered, then. What it would be like to actually live with a man? To have one in her life? In her home? In her bed?

And just like that she was fantasizing about Knox in her bed…

Don't miss
THE RANCHER'S BABY
by New York Times *bestselling author Maisey Yates,*
the first book in the **TEXAS CATTLEMAN'S CLUB:**
THE IMPOSTOR *series! Available January 2018*
wherever Harlequin® Desire books and ebooks are sold.

And then follow the whole saga—
Will the scandal of the century lead to love for these rich ranchers?
The Rancher's Baby by New York Times *bestselling author Maisey Yates*
Rich Rancher's Redemption by USA TODAY *bestselling author Maureen Child*
A Convenient Texas Wedding by Sheri WhiteFeather
Expecting a Scandal by Joanne Rock
Reunited…with Baby by USA TODAY *bestselling author Sara Orwig*
The Nanny Proposal by Joss Wood
Secret Twins for the Texan by Karen Booth
Lone Star Secrets by Cat Schield

www.Harlequin.com

LOVE
Harlequin
romance?

Join our Harlequin community to share your thoughts and connect with other romance readers!

Be the first to find out about promotions, news, and exclusive content!

Sign up for the Harlequin e-newsletter and download a free book from any series at

www.TryHarlequin.com

CONNECT WITH US AT:

Harlequin.com/Community

 Facebook.com/HarlequinBooks

Twitter.com/HarlequinBooks

Instagram.com/HarlequinBooks

Pinterest.com/HarlequinBooks

ReaderService.com

 **HARLEQUIN®**

**ROMANCE WHEN
YOU NEED IT**

HSOCIAL2017

Want to give in to temptation with steamy tales of irresistible desire?

Check out **Harlequin® Presents®, Harlequin® Desire** and **Harlequin® Kimani™ Romance** books!

New books available every month!

CONNECT WITH US AT:

Harlequin.com/Community

 Facebook.com/HarlequinBooks

Twitter.com/HarlequinBooks

Instagram.com/HarlequinBooks

Pinterest.com/HarlequinBooks

ReaderService.com

**ROMANCE WHEN
YOU NEED IT**

THE WORLD IS BETTER
WITH
Romance

Harlequin has everything from contemporary, passionate and heartwarming to suspenseful and inspirational stories.

Whatever your mood,
we have a romance just for you!

Connect with us to find your next great read, special offers and more.

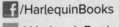

/HarlequinBooks

@HarlequinBooks

www.HarlequinBlog.com

www.Harlequin.com/Newsletters

HARLEQUIN®

A *Romance* FOR EVERY MOOD™

www.Harlequin.com

HARLEQUIN®

A *Romance* FOR EVERY MOOD™

Love the Harlequin book you just read?

Your opinion matters.

Review this book on your favorite book site, review site, blog or your own social media properties and share your opinion with other readers!

Be sure to connect with us at:
Harlequin.com/Newsletters
Facebook.com/HarlequinBooks
Twitter.com/HarlequinBooks